USBORNE

Sandy
Lane
Stables

Racing Vacation

Michelle Bates

USBORNE

First published in 2000 by Usborne Publishing Ltd, Usborne House,
83-85 Saffron Hill, London EC1N 8RT, England.
www.usborne.com

First published in America 2000. AE

A catalogue record for this title is available from the British Library.

ISBN 07945 0504 X (paperback)

Typeset in Times

Printed in Great Britain

Edited by: Jenny Tyler
Designed by: Lucy Parris
Cover Design: Neil Francis
Map Illustrations: John Woodcock
Cover Photograph supplied by: Only Horses

CONTENTS

Training Oval / Racetrack

Graytops Horse Farm

Ted Bailey's Apartment →

Yearlings' Corral

Horse Barn

Tack Room

Office

Horse Barn

Stable Yard

Coral Berry Avenue

To Airport

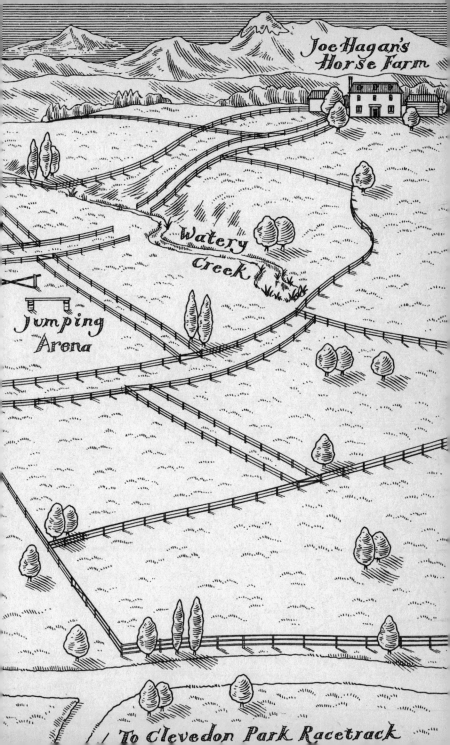

Joe Hagan's Horse Farm

Watery Creek

Jumping Arena

To Clevedon Park Racetrack

1

SANDY LANE STABLES

"I can't believe we're actually going – a three week vacation in Kentucky and with all the riding we could possibly want!" Izzy Paterson stood in the middle of the yard at Sandy Lane Stables, a big grin stretching from ear to ear.

"I know, I can hardly believe it myself," Kate Hardy answered, her white-blonde hair contrasting dramatically with the dark bay coat of the pony she was grooming. "It's the vacation of a lifetime!"

That was what all the Sandy Lane regulars had said when they'd first heard Nick and Sarah Brooks, the stable owners, talk about the riding vacation they'd arranged as the prize for the Sandy Lane Christmas raffle. And now, here stood Izzy and Kate, on the first day of the summer vacation, with just a week left to go until they'd be boarding the plane.

The vacation of a lifetime... the words rang in

Izzy's ears. Sarah had talked a lot about the place they'd be staying, and it sounded amazing – the Graytops Horse Farm for racehorses, tucked deep in the rolling countryside. Sarah had known the owners, Doug and Sally Bryant, since childhood and was godmother to their twin daughters, Megan and Courtney. Izzy and Kate were going to live and ride with the family, and in return, the twins would come to Sandy Lane the following summer. Everything was going to be just perfect.

"Oh Izzy, what's the matter?" Kate couldn't help but notice the sad look flash across her friend's face.

"It's nothing really," Izzy said, running a hand through her dark curls. "If only-"

"If only what?" Kate looked puzzled.

"If only I didn't have to leave Midnight behind, that's all." Izzy turned away, feeling a little choked as she looked at the sleek, black horse standing behind her. "I guess you could say it's the only downside of the trip."

"Oh Izzy." Kate didn't know what to say. "But you've known all along that you couldn't take him with you."

"I know, I know," Izzy sighed. "Only I didn't realize how bad I'd feel when I was actually faced with leaving him."

"But he'll be in good hands here at Sandy Lane," Kate stepped in quickly. "And three weeks will fly by – before you know it, we'll be back in Virginia and wishing we were still in Kentucky. And think of all the stories you'll have to tell him when you get back."

"That's true," Izzy giggled, instantly feeling better.

"And Rosie's agreed to ride him at the Colcott Show next weekend, so he won't be missing out on anything."

"You see?" Kate went on. "It's going to be all right. You couldn't *not* go on this trip. And now look, here's a sight that should bring a smile to your face."

Izzy turned and looked across the yard to where Kate was pointing. There was Rosie, coming out of the tack room, a bridle slung over her shoulder and a whole load of things gathered in her arms – saddle, crop, riding hat, brushes. Nick and Sarah's black labrador, Ebony, trailed along behind her, wagging his tail.

"I give her ten seconds before she drops something," Izzy chuckled, drawing her sweater in tighter around her. It might have been summer, but there was a cool nip in the air that morning.

"Hey, you two, how's it going?" Rosie called as she walked on up to them. "Now, let me guess what you're talking about – could it be *Kentucky* perhaps?"

"You guessed it," Kate grinned.

"Well, I don't blame you." Rosie stopped beside them and dumped the saddle down. The brushes slid to the floor. "Oops..." Rosie bent down to pick them up. "You must be pretty excited about this vacation by now. Do you mind if I take over, Izzy?" She nodded in Midnight's direction.

"No, of course I don't mind," Izzy answered. "After all, I've got high hopes for you and Midnight this year – you're going to be carrying off that Colcott Open Jumping trophy for me."

"Well, I don't know about that," Rosie smiled, looking pleased. "But I'll certainly do my best." Then

3

she turned back to Kate. "I hear you got another letter from Courtney and Megan this morning. What did they have to say?"

"Well." Kate pulled a letter out of her pocket. "Shall I read it out loud while you're tacking up?"

"Sure," Rosie said.

Kate took a deep breath. "In the words of Courtney Bryant: *Hi you guys, how's it going in Virginia? It's been pretty awful at school with our final exams and stuff...*"

"Oh, don't bother with the boring parts," Izzy jumped in.

"Patience," Kate said, feigning an angry look as she went on. "*The farm is looking great. We've been taking Garnet and Prince-*"

"Those are their ponies," Izzy interrupted, leaning over Kate's shoulder.

"Are you going to let me get on with this, or what?" Kate said indignantly. Izzy poked out her tongue and grinned and quickly Kate buried herself back in the letter. "*We've been taking Garnet and Prince to the creek to swim, but they don't really do much more than paddle because Garnet is afraid of the water and Prince won't do anything by himself.*

...It's really busy on the farm right now – what with all the race meets coming up. Things have been so crazy, but we'll fill you in on everything when you get here. You're probably more interested in hearing about all of the riding you'll be doing than our business, and don't you worry, there'll be plenty of that. We'll have to take turns riding Garnet and Prince, but Mom has been talking to Nick and she seems to think you'll be up to working some of the

4

racehorses too – well, the less spirited ones anyway."

"Did you get that?" Izzy joined in excitedly. "We'll be riding *real* racehorses."

"*That's all we've got time for now, guys,*" Kate finished off the letter. "*So we'll see you both on the 2nd. Can't wait to meet you. Love Courtney and Megan.*" Kate looked up expectantly.

"Well, it does all sound wonderful." Rosie looked wistful. "I'd be feeling really left out if it wasn't for the Colcott Show."

"Speaking of the Colcott Show – look who's on his way over." Kate nudged Rosie and the three girls looked across the yard to see Tom Buchanan striding toward them.

"Uh oh, I guess I'd better get a move on." Rosie went to duck under Izzy's arm.

"Not so quick." Izzy grabbed her back. "Tom doesn't run the stables, you know."

"Though you'd never guess it these days," Kate muttered under her breath.

Tom was the star rider at Sandy Lane, only now he was training to be a riding instructor as well. He had taken over the jumping practices for the summer shows which helped take the pressure off Nick.

"Hey you guys... haven't you got anything better to do than just stand around gossiping?" Tom's voice echoed around the yard, breaking up the conversation.

"Here we go again," Kate muttered.

"Jumping practice is in ten minutes, Rosie," he reminded her.

"Don't worry, I'll be there." Rosie looked at her friend and raised her eyebrows. "I guess I'd better get a move on."

5

"Yeah, yeah," Izzy said. "In your own time."

"Oh come on, Izzy," Kate said plaintively. "Winding Tom up simply isn't worth it."

"Did you hear what I said, Rosie?" Tom called back across the yard. "Oh by the way – Izzy... Kate, I'm afraid there isn't room for you in today's practice."

"Oh what?" Izzy groaned.

"I've already got ten riders," Tom went on. "And you know that Nick doesn't like me taking more than that in a group."

"But-" Izzy started.

"No buts," Tom jumped in quickly. "You know the rules – the first ones to sign up get priority."

"But you must have known we'd want to join in," Kate wheedled. "I mean, I know we're not competing at Colcott, but we are regular riders at Sandy Lane."

"Maybe," Tom shrugged. "But that doesn't give you automatic entry to my practices." And with that, Tom was gone.

"Of all the patronizing, smug..." Izzy was fuming.

"Oh come on, Izzy." Rosie jumped to Tom's defense. "Tom is under a lot of pressure at the moment, with his instructor's exams coming up and everything."

"I suppose so," Izzy said, though she didn't look entirely convinced. "But ever since he's taken up this teaching business he's been a complete nightmare."

"You can say that again," Kate agreed.

"I'm sure he'll be back to his old self soon enough." Rosie shrugged her shoulders.

"Maybe." Izzy nodded and, giving Midnight one final pat, she moved away. "Come on then, Kate."

The stables were busy as the two girls made their

way across the yard – riders were dashing this way and that, and horses were stamping their feet in anticipation of the ride ahead.

"You know, Tom always seems to pick on Rosie these days," Kate finally spoke up. "It wouldn't surprise me if he had a little crush on her."

"Well, he's got a funny way of showing it if he does," Izzy said.

"I know, but boys aren't exactly the easiest creatures to understand, are they?" Kate wrinkled up her brow. "Take my brother as an example – I never know what Alex is thinking."

"Well, if you ask me this vacation couldn't have come at a better time," Izzy said, quickly changing the subject. She and Alex had become more than just friends at Christmas, but that had all fizzled out now and she didn't like talking about him. "If I thought I was going to have to take lessons from Tom all summer, I'd end up going crazy."

Kate nodded. "Three weeks on a Kentucky horse farm or jumping practices with the bossiest person in the world – not much of a choice, eh? Now come on, let's go and see if Nick and Sarah have time to talk about Graytops. Not even Tom's nagging can get to me right now."

"Me neither," Izzy said. "Six more days to go – I don't know how I'll get through them."

"Don't you worry," Kate grinned. "We'll manage."

2

THEY'RE OFF!

The week actually passed quicker than either Izzy or Kate could have thought possible – what with all the time spent riding at Sandy Lane, and then shopping for their trip. It seemed like no time at all before Saturday was upon them, and they were piling their bags into Izzy's mother's car. They were off to the airport. It wasn't until they were sitting on the plane, though, that either of them felt able to believe they were really going.

Kate leaned back in her seat. "Well, checking-in was easier than I thought."

"Told you so." Izzy looked nonchalant as she munched her way through a bag of peanuts. "Traveling's a breeze."

"That's all right for you to say," Kate frowned, opening her horse magazine. "You might have traveled lots, but this is only my third trip on a plane."

Izzy grinned. "Oh Kate, come on, don't read, let's talk."

"We've got plenty of time for talking," Kate laughed. "We have got three whole weeks together."

"Hmm, but we'll be riding racehorses for most of that," Izzy sighed, putting her hands behind her head and yawning. "What with all the mucking out and grooming I've been doing this week, I'm exhausted. Nick sure has gotten a lot of work out of me."

"Yes, but he is keeping Midnight on at Sandy Lane for free," Kate reminded her.

"And don't I know it!" Izzy raised her eyebrows.

"Anyway," Kate started. "Enough about Sandy Lane; what time do we get to Graytops?"

"About ten o'clock tonight," Izzy said promptly. "That's nine o'clock Virginia time."

"And it's a two hour drive from the airport?" Kate questioned her.

"Yes," Izzy answered impatiently.

"And the Bryants did say they'd meet us?"

"Of course they did, Kate," Izzy said, beginning to sound impatient. "Stop worrying."

"All right, all right." Kate was defensive. "I just wanted to make sure, that's all. So what do you think Graytops'll be like?"

"Everything we expect and more," Izzy sighed. "Paddocks upon paddocks of grassy fields, birds soaring in the bright blue sky, crickets chirping in the night, day after day of riding in the sun, horses kicking up dusty trails..."

"You have a vivid imagination, Izzy," Kate laughed.

"Well that's what happens when you've got an

author for a dad," Izzy answered quickly. "Now look
– there's a movie about to start." She pointed at the
screen in front of them.

"Oh great!" Kate exclaimed, digging into the seat
pocket and grabbing her earphones.

"Wake me up when we get there." Izzy reclined
her seat and shut her eyes.

Kate raised her eyes skyward. "Was there anything
else, Madam?"

*

"Would all passengers from flight AA 123 from
Norfolk International proceed to Baggage Claim Zone
B?" a voice announced over the intercom.

"That's us." Kate nudged Izzy excitedly. "The
sooner we get our bags, the sooner we'll be at
Graytops."

Impatiently, Izzy and Kate hurried to the
baggage claim to where the conveyor belt was
going around and around. Suitcases, duffle bags,
backpacks, boxes... but none of them seemed to
be theirs.

"I hope our bags haven't gotten lost," Kate
muttered anxiously.

"Of course they're not lost," Izzy said calmly.

But when Kate's bag came out with the next load,
and Izzy's was nowhere to be seen, it was Izzy who
began to lose her cool.

"Where can it have gone?" she wailed. "It's got
everything in it – my jodhs, my favorite baggy black

jumper."

"Oh Izzy," Kate laughed. "It'll be here in a minute. Look, isn't that it over there? The one with the big horse sticker on the side?"

"Yes, that's it," Izzy said, feeling relieved as her black duffle bag came around the corner. She dumped it down on the cart and spun around. "All right, let's go."

The automatic doors swung open, and Izzy and Kate found themselves staring at a sea of faces.

"I feel like royalty," Izzy whispered.

"I know, embarrassing, isn't it?" Kate felt nervous as they made their way down the walkway. "Can you see anyone who looks like the Bryants?"

"No, I don't think I can."

Izzy took a quick look around her as they reached the end. "You wait here and I'll have a quick look around."

Two minutes later, Izzy was back at Kate's side. "I can't see any of them anywhere."

"Maybe they've been delayed," Kate shrugged. "I'm sure they'll be here in a moment."

"But what will we do if they don't come?" Izzy wrinkled up her brow in a worried expression. "Should we call home?"

"No, I don't think we can do that," Kate said slowly. "We'll try and call Graytops. But hang on a minute, who's that over there?"

Izzy looked in the direction Kate was pointing to where a man stood by himself, holding a sign. The writing on it was small, but now that she looked more closely, she could see that it had their names on it.

"That must be Mr. Bryant – how could we have missed him?" Kate whispered.

"Maybe because we were expecting the whole family to turn up?" Izzy muttered. "Come on, let's go over."

Pushing the cart forward, Kate and Izzy walked across to the man to introduce themselves.

"Mr. Bryant?" Kate said tentatively. "I'm Kate Hardy and this is Izzy Paterson."

"Oh right, well, first of all – I'm not Mr. Bryant," the man said. "I'm just your taxi driver."

Kate and Izzy exchanged surprised glances. "Oh, uh, right, we thought the Bryants were going to be picking us up," Izzy said.

"Dunno anything about that," the taxi driver answered. "I was just booked to pick you up. So where are you girls from?"

"Virginia," Izzy said, starting to feel a little lost.

"Near Richmond?" the man asked.

"Not exactly," Kate answered.

Then there was an awkward moment when no one seemed to know what to say to each other. Finally the taxi driver spoke up. "Well, let's go then." And, grabbing their cart, he made for the doors.

As he disappeared off into the distance, Izzy and Kate looked warily at each other.

"Do you think this is all right, Izzy?" Kate said.

"I guess so." Izzy looked uncertain. "But don't you think it's a little weird? I mean, the Bryants did say they'd be here."

"I know they did," Kate murmured. "But I'm sure there'll be a reasonable explanation when we get to Graytops." She looked ahead of her to where the driver had stopped and was now waiting. "I think we should follow him, or we might find ourselves stranded at the airport..."

*

It was dark when the taxi turned off a main road. Kate sat, wide-eyed, as they drove through the big iron gates. Quickly, she nudged Izzy, asleep at her side. *'Graytops Horse Farm',* read the sign.

"Izzy... Izzy, I think we're here," she murmured, not wanting to startle her sleeping friend.

"What?" Izzy mumbled, her head nodding forward.

"We're here," Kate said, nudging her again as the car sped up the driveway.

"Here? Where?" Izzy sat bolt upright.

"We've arrived."

"Oh right," Izzy grunted. "I must have fallen asleep."

"You can say that again, you were sawing logs in your sleep." Kate laughed as the car drove up to a grassy cul-de-sac and stopped by a big, white house with gray, sloping roofs.

"It's larger than I expected," Kate whispered, looking out of her window.

"And it looks very different than the houses back home," Izzy murmured sleepily. "It's huge."

"Here you are then," the driver interrupted their conversation, getting out of the taxi and going around to the trunk. Izzy and Kate pushed open their car doors and stepped outside. The sultry hot night air was the first thing to hit them – after the cool of the air-conditioned taxi it was like stepping into a sauna.

"Whew, it's baking out here." Izzy waved her hand around in front of her face.

Kate nodded, feeling equally frazzled as the driver deposited the bags at their side.

"Taxi's all paid for, so I'll be going. Enjoy your vacation."

"Oh right, well thanks," Izzy said.

Izzy and Kate picked up their bags and made their way up the steps to the front door of the house.

"Where's the doorbell?" Izzy hissed.

"Here," Kate answered, reaching up to push an ornate button. She took a step back.

"It's lovely and peaceful, isn't it?" Izzy said, looking around her.

"Yes it is," Kate said. "It looks like we're completely in the middle of nowhere."

Patiently, Izzy and Kate stood there, waiting. Finally Izzy took a step forward and looked in through the side window. "You know, there aren't any lights on in there."

"Well, I wish they'd get a move on," Kate said. "I want my bed."

"Same here." Izzy nodded. She peered in through the window again. "You know, I don't think there's anyone at home."

"There must be," Kate said, pushing the doorbell again.

"Maybe we should go and take a look over there." Izzy turned and looked to the left of the house, pointing in the direction of some lights in the distance.

"Okay." Kate shoved her bag under a bench by the

door and followed Izzy's lead across the grass. As they reached the trees, they came to a track. The lights seemed to be getting further away and it seemed to be getting darker and darker.

"Spooky, isn't it?" Izzy shivered as they headed forward.

"Yes, but we'll be all right," Kate said, glancing up at the overhanging branches.

"I think I can hear voices," Izzy said. "Ahead of us... listen." She grabbed Kate by the arm and they drew to a halt.

"I can't hear a thing," Kate murmured.

"I feel kind of funny about this," Izzy said. "It seems weird – like we're tres-"

And then there was a voice from behind them that cut Izzy's sentence off short.

"Hey you two – what do you think you're doing?"

Izzy and Kate spun around in their tracks, their hearts pounding.

3

A STRANGE BEGINNING

It was so dark that it was difficult to see where the voice was coming from, but then, as Izzy and Kate stood rooted to the spot, they saw a flashlight coming from their right.

"Well, who are you?" The voice came again. It was a man's voice and he sounded angry.

"We're... we're..." Kate stuttered, stumbling for the right words as the man appeared, standing in front of them. He was dressed in some kind of uniform and had a dog on a leash by his side. He didn't look like he could be one of the Bryants.

Kate found her voice. "We're Kate Hardy and Izzy Paterson. We've come to stay."

"To stay?" The man's voice still sounded suspicious, but at least it had softened a little. The dog at his side growled.

"We've come for three weeks," Izzy piped up. "We

16

couldn't find anybody at the house."

"No, they're all over at the stables," the man answered gruffly.

Izzy and Kate waited, not knowing whether they should go on or not. And then the man lifted his hand and jerked it back behind him. "You've taken a wrong turn off the track. I'd take you over there, but I'm too busy. If you head to your right, you'll get there. When the track divides in two, take the left-hand fork and then go straight. That'll bring you to the entrance of the stables."

"Er, thank you, thanks a lot," Kate said.

"And don't go wandering off again," the man shouted after them.

"No, we won't," Izzy answered.

"Strange," Kate shivered as the man slipped away into the darkness. "I suppose he must be a security guard."

"Even so, you'd have thought he'd have been told we were coming, wouldn't you?" Izzy said, biting on her bottom lip as they made their way back to where they'd just come from.

"Yes, you would," Kate said, feeling strangely forlorn. No one at the airport to greet them; no one at the house when they arrived; the unfriendly man – none of it added up to make either of them feel very welcome and, as they headed nearer and nearer the stable yard, they felt really unsettled.

"Stop a minute." Izzy held out her arm.

"Why? What is it?" Kate answered.

"There, up ahead," Izzy said. "Voices... can you hear them?"

"I think I can," Kate said slowly. "Angry voices,

and look – what are all those people doing?"

Kate stepped forward and strained her eyes to see. It was dark, but she could just make out an archway and, beyond that, a yard. A trailer stood with its ramp down, and there was a group of people crowded around it. A man looked to be trying to load up a horse and a pale-haired woman by his side was trying to grab the lead rope from him.

"Seems a little strange," Kate said. "Why do you think they're transporting horses at night?"

"Oh Kate," Izzy laughed. "It's hardly strange. This is a racing stables."

"I suppose so," Kate shrugged as they walked under the cover of the trees. When they were within fifty paces of the lights they stopped. The horse had been led up into the box now and the group of people stood, talking heatedly.

"We wouldn't do anything like that. Give us the benefit of the doubt..."

"If you take him away now it could ruin everything..."

"We'll get to the bottom of this, it'll be all right..."

Izzy and Kate could just catch snippets of the conversation.

"Come on, let's go over to them," Kate said. "I feel funny just listening in."

Izzy nodded. They waited for a moment as the trailer backed through the archway, the flash of the headlights lighting up the trees, then quickly they walked forward.

Everyone was so busy in discussion that it wasn't until they were nearly upon the group that anyone noticed them. Then, a couple of voices called out.

18

"Hey Mom, it's Izzy and Kate... they're here already." Two girls rushed to greet them. "How did you get here so quickly? Are you tired? How was the flight?"

Izzy smiled tentatively, looking from one girl to the other.

"Sorry, I guess we'd better start by introducing ourselves." One of the girls laughed and stepped forward. "I'm Courtney and this is Megan."

Izzy was confused. At first glance, you'd have thought that the two girls were identical in every way. Both of them had long, red hair, and bright green eyes, but now that she looked more closely, she realized that the girl who'd said she was Courtney was slightly taller than the other one.

"Well, hello there." The woman who'd been struggling with the horse walked over to them. "It's good to see you both." She was smiling, but her voice sounded weary. "I'm Mrs. Bryant, but you can call me Sally. Welcome to Graytops. I'm sorry we couldn't be there to meet you at the airport but something came up and... well anyway, I guess you must be pretty tired after all that traveling. Let's get you over to the house and settle you in."

"Aw, Mom." Was it Courtney? Or was it Megan? Neither Izzy or Kate could be sure, but one of the girls started talking. "Izzy and Kate'll want to look at the horses first."

"Tomorrow, girls, tomorrow," Sally Bryant laughed. "I know you're excited, but it's getting late and Kate and Izzy have had a long day – I'm sure they'll want to get to bed."

"I never thought I'd hear myself say I'd rather sleep

than see horses!" Izzy turned to look at Kate. "But I'm dead on my feet."

"Me too," Kate nodded and sighed.

Izzy and Kate didn't need any further encouragement and happily they followed Sally's lead... back along the track, through the trees, and across the grass to the house. As they walked, Courtney and Megan chattered away nineteen to the dozen – all about the horses; what they'd been doing that day; all the stuff they had planned for the weeks ahead. They hardly stopped to draw breath, but at least it made Izzy and Kate feel more at ease.

"Well, here we are then," Sally said finally as they reached the steps of the house. "Courtney... Megan, can you bring up Izzy and Kate's bags? I'm just going to go on up and get their bedroom ready."

"Oh, we can manage our bags," Kate said quickly.

"Don't you worry about that." Sally raised her arm. "The girls can do it. Now, come with me."

"Well, if you're sure..." Kate and Izzy were too weary to protest and so they turned to follow Sally through the house. It was as cool as a refrigerator inside, and good to be out of the heat. The house was furnished in bright reds and oranges which gave it a warm feel. As they climbed the wooden staircase, they noticed all of the photographs on the walls – *'Seattle Surprise winning the Ashworth Maiden Stakes,'* read one of them. *'Doug Bryant being presented with the bowl for best new trainer,'* read another.

It was at that point that it suddenly occurred to Kate that they had neither met the twins' father, nor heard mention of him.

"Will Mr. Bryant be back soon?" Kate asked, glancing over her shoulder at the photos.

"Uh, well no. Actually, he's not staying here right now," Sally answered vaguely. "In fact, he'll probably be away for most of your visit. Now, here we are." As they arrived at a twin-bedded room, she quickly changed the subject. Izzy gave Kate a look that said *'that's strange'* but now Sally was talking again.

"Oh no, I've completely forgotten to make up your beds. How stupid of me. Look, would you mind doing it yourselves?"

"No, of course not, that's fine," Izzy said, trying not to sound too surprised.

"Thank you," Sally said gratefully. "It's been a long day and I'm absolutely exhausted." Sally looked weary as she walked across the room to the window and drew the curtains across... just as Courtney and Megan deposited Izzy and Kate's bags inside the door. They all looked a little awkward as they stood there.

"Okay girls..." Sally broke the uncomfortable silence and turned to Izzy and Kate. "I think you'll enjoy the view from this room. You can see for miles – right across the paddocks to the hills beyond. Now if you need anything, I'm just at the end of the hall and the girls are next door." She opened a door and showed them an en-suite bathroom. "Come on Courtney and Megan... bedtime. I'll just go and get some bed sheets for Izzy and Kate."

"Good night, Courtney, good night, Megan." Izzy let out a loud yawn.

"Good night," the twins responded. "See you in the morning."

As soon as the bedroom door was closed behind

them, Izzy turned to Kate. "So where do you think Mr. Bryant is?" she hissed. "It's a little strange, isn't it?"

"I suppose so," Kate shrugged. "Maybe they're having marital problems. You never know-"

"Ssshh," Izzy whispered. "I can hear her coming back."

"Well, here we are – sheets and pillowcases." Sally pushed back the door and dropped the pile onto the nearest bed. "I think that's everything so I'll leave you to get ready."

"Oh right, er, so what time should we get up for breakfast?" Izzy asked hesitantly.

"Oh, just whenever you're awake." Sally rubbed her brow. "Anyway, good night, and sleep well, girls."

And with that, she closed the door behind her.

Izzy stood still for a moment, watching as Kate wandered into the bathroom. Then she picked up a sheet and started making up her bed. "It's all very laid back here, isn't it?" she said. "And don't you think it's a little strange that no one explained why they weren't at the airport to meet us? And why do you think Sally didn't make the beds up earlier? They don't seem very prepared, do they? My mom would never have forgotten something like that."

"No, neither would mine." Kate stood in the doorway to the bathroom, brushing her teeth. "But then maybe Sally's got more on her plate than our moms." Kate raised her eyebrows as she came back out of the bathroom. She looked quizzically at the sheets.

"Here, let me show you how to do it." Izzy grabbed Kate's bottom sheet and waved it out in the air.

Quickly, she put the pillowcases on Kate's pillows and tucked everything in before hopping into her own bed. "So, is it what you expected here then?"

"Well no, not exactly," Kate answered. "But Courtney and Megan are friendly which sort of makes up for it... I've never seen anyone look so disappointed when we said we wanted to go to bed rather than meet the horses, and Sally – well, if she's having marital problems... Izzy, Izzy, can you hear me?"

But there wasn't any reply to her question and it was only when Kate listened carefully and heard her friend's rhythmic breathing that she realized that Izzy had dozed off – and just as she was talking! Kate lay back on her pillow, letting the thoughts run through her mind. She was sure that a good night's sleep would make everything seem much more normal in the morning. And, closing her eyes, she snuggled down into her bed. It wasn't long before she too was sleeping soundly.

4

GRAYTOPS HORSE FARM

When Kate and Izzy woke the next morning and saw the farm from their bedroom window, all of their concerns from the previous night were instantly forgotten. It looked wonderful – acres upon acres of white-railed paddocks stretched before their eyes. Tall lime trees blew in the breeze and in the distance a watery creek shimmered in the morning sunshine.

"Wow!" Izzy sighed. "It's great!"

"Isn't it?" Kate smiled contentedly. "Look over there."

Izzy looked to where Kate was pointing – a large oval-shaped paddock lay ahead of them on which horses with riders were galloping around.

"Look at that gray mare," Kate breathed. "Isn't she beautiful?"

"Isn't she just?" Izzy sighed.

"I guess it must be some kind of training track."

Izzy jumped down off the window seat. "Let's get down there and take a look."

Quickly the two girls showered and dressed before hurrying down the hall. The doors to the other rooms stood open on each side. Kate poked her head around one of them and called out. "Hello in there..." But there was no answer. Kate and Izzy hurried on, past another empty room and turned the corner of the hallway. As they reached the bottom of the stairs, Izzy looked around her. "Doesn't look as though there's anybody here."

"What do you think we should do?" Kate walked into the kitchen. "Breakfast's been laid out – maybe we should just help ourselves?"

"Can you see a note or anything?" Izzy looked around her.

"No, nothing," Kate said. "Look, it's eight-thirty already – they're probably all over at the barn. Let's leave breakfast for now and go and find them."

"All right," Izzy said.

And so the two girls left the house, making their way off across the grass. Glancing left, they caught sight of the security guard pacing around the grounds, but by daylight he didn't seem nearly as scary. Quickening their pace, they headed down the path through the trees and turned the corner to the stables. There ahead of them stood the arched entrance to the stable yard.

It was already pretty busy – horses were being led in through the back gate and jockeys were dismounting. The noise of people talking and horses neighing made a loud commotion.

It had been hard to see what the stables really

looked like last night but now, lit by the morning sun, the farm stood in its full glory. There were two large whitewashed barns standing opposite each other, a tack room, and at the top of the graveled yard a red-brick building which looked as though it might be an office. Izzy and Kate were just wondering where to go when Sally appeared from one of the barns and called across to them.

"Hi there, you two. Come on over."

Gladly, Izzy and Kate zigzagged across the yard, avoiding the backsides of the various horses.

"You've arrived right at our busiest time," Sally said. "The exercise string has just come in from training, but don't worry, the yard will clear in a minute. This bunch'll be leaving soon." She waved her hands around. "Most of the exercise riders are only here for an hour. They'll be on to the next stables after that."

"Sally... Sally... over here!"

The two girls spun around to see a man walking over to them. He was small and thick-set with gray hair and a wizened face... roughly in his mid-fifties.

"Can you take a look at Seattle Surprise, Sally?" the man said. "She's limping a little."

"Oh no," Sally groaned. "That's all we need. Okay, I'll be right there. By the way, these are our guests, Izzy and Kate," she said, indicating the two girls. "Do you remember me mentioning the girls coming in from Virginia?"

"Oh yeah, yeah I do," the little man grunted and turned away. Before Izzy and Kate had a chance to say anything, he had disappeared off across the yard.

"Well, that was our stable manager, Ted Bailey,"

26

Sally said distractedly.

"Oh right." Izzy and Kate looked at each other, not quite knowing what to say.

"Don't worry if he's a little unfriendly," Sally went on. "He spends most of his time around horses... doesn't know how to talk to people. Still, he's one-hundred percent reliable, which is more than can be said for some of the stable managers we've had. Now, why don't you go and look for Courtney and Megan? They'll be in that barn over there."

"Wow, it's a lot more hectic than Sandy Lane." Izzy raised her eyebrows as Sally rushed away and they walked over to the barn.

It was cool as they stepped inside and both girls were glad to be out of the morning sun. Inside, the building was divided into two rows with five stalls on either side, and an aisle running down the middle.

"You made it!" A voice cried out from the end stall. Kate and Izzy weren't sure whether the face that appeared was Courtney's or Megan's. Then another face appeared alongside, so it didn't really matter – the twins stepped out into the aisle.

"Are you ready for your guided tour?" one of them asked.

"You bet!" Izzy and Kate answered in unison.

Courtney and Megan led Izzy and Kate out of the building and across the stable yard.

"How many horses do you have here then?" Izzy asked, jogging to keep up.

"Fifteen," Megan answered promptly. "But some of them are too young to race yet."

The four girls walked into the next horse barn. "And here are our ponies – Prince and Garnet," Megan

27

said as they stopped at the end of the aisle. Izzy and Kate looked over each of the stalls to see two lovely-looking ponies – a chestnut with two white socks, and a big, bay pony, with fine black markings and large brown eyes.

Courtney drew back the bolt on the door and stepped into the stall. "How are you feeling, buddy?" she crooned, tickling Prince behind his ears. Then she turned to Izzy and Kate. "We should take them out to the paddocks to graze. Do you want to grab Garnet?"

"Sure." Kate drew back the bolt to the chestnut's stall and, taking the lead-rope from the hook on the wall, she clipped it onto his headcollar. Then she led him out.

Courtney and Kate led the ponies across the gravel until they reached the back gate. Then they let Garnet and Prince off their lead ropes. The ponies ambled away – just a few feet from them – and started nibbling at the grass.

Courtney grinned fondly at the two ponies. Then she turned and pointed to the paddock on the right of them. "Those are the new yearlings. We've taken three on in training this year."

"Look at the speed of them," Kate breathed as she watched two colts and a filly kick up their heels and set a blazing trail across the grass.

Most of the horses had been taken off to be rubbed down by the time the girls turned back to the yard. Megan and Courtney took Izzy and Kate into the next horse barn and led them down the line of racehorses, pointing each one out by name and giving them a brief potted history of all of the races they'd run in.

Izzy looked into a stall at a beautiful black stallion – sleek and polished with a long white blaze. "Wow!" She reached in to pat his neck, turning back around to talk to Courtney and Megan at the same time. "How old is he? Eeek!" She jumped back in surprise as the horse went to take a chunk out of her arm.

"Well, you've just met Fiery Lad," Courtney chuckled. "He's kind of temperamental to say the least."

"I don't think he likes you, Izzy," Kate laughed.

Izzy ignored the remark and stepped forward again to pat his neck. This time, much to her relief, he didn't move a muscle.

"He's magnificent," she breathed, trying to ignore the fact that Fiery Lad was still baring his teeth at her. But the others had already moved on. Kate had stopped at the backside of a gray mare and was looking her up and down appreciatively. "This one's gorgeous."

Izzy joined them and took in the long straight legs and gentle sloping shoulders of the creature standing before her.

"Well, you've got a good eye," Courtney grinned. "That's Seattle Surprise – our best racehorse. She's already won a couple of good races for us this season."

"Oh yes, your mom had to go and check her out earlier," Kate said. "She was limping or something."

"No way!" Courtney groaned. "That's all we need with her big race coming up."

"She's prepping for the Gresham Maiden Stakes at Clevedon Park Racetrack in a couple of weeks,"

Megan explained. "It's a pretty important race for us – the purse is worth $100,000."

"Amazing." Izzy's eyes nearly popped out of her head.

"So who owns all of your horses?" Kate asked.

"Well," Courtney started. "We own some of them ourselves – Seattle Surprise, for instance – but the rest are owned by different people. We usually make our money from being trainers instead of owners."

"It's no wonder you need the security guard with such valuable horses around then," Izzy joined in.

It was an innocent statement, said more as a way of making conversation than anything else, but Courtney seemed to be suspicious. "Security guard? Where did you see him? What did he say to you?" Courtney spoke sharply.

"Well, we saw him last night," Izzy stammered. "And he didn't say very much – other than scare us half out of our wits." She tried to make a joke out of a potentially awkward situation. "He didn't seem to know who we were."

"Oh, okay." Courtney's tone relaxed. "I guess Mom must have forgotten to tell him you were coming. Look, I didn't mean to bite your head off – it's just that he's meant to be kind of a secret, that's all."

"Oh, I see." Izzy shrugged and nodded. A security guard who was *meant to be kind of a secret*? That sounded somewhat silly to her, but judging from Courtney's manner, it was best not to say anything.

"Training farms always keep a security guard around," Megan joined in, looking embarrassed.

"Oh I'm sure they do," Kate said, not wanting an argument breaking out over something that didn't

30

seem very important.

"Anyway, shall we get going?" Megan said.

"That would be great... fantastic!" Izzy exclaimed.

To any other person it would have just sounded like Izzy was being over-enthusiastic, but Kate knew that Izzy wasn't the sort of person to get over-enthusiastic about anything. She was clearly trying to make up for what had happened back there. And while Kate understood her friend's reasoning, she didn't necessarily think that Izzy was right to take the back foot when she hadn't said or done anything wrong. Courtney had just acted so defensive – without any provocation at all – and that, Kate thought, was totally out of line.

5

THE HARD WORK BEGINS

Kate and Izzy found themselves rushed off their feet that Sunday afternoon. If they weren't organizing feeds or grooming horses, they were changing water-buckets or cleaning tack. Still, they weren't complaining – not when they were around the animals they loved most in the world. It was only when Sally said it was time for supper and they made their way over to the house that they suddenly realized how tired they were feeling.

"So how was your day?" Sally said as they sat down at the kitchen table.

"Exhausting," Kate answered.

"Well, you've made a good start at Graytops," Sally said, looking pretty tired herself. "And thanks for all your help. We'll have to organize a real schedule for tomorrow." She raised a fork of salad to her mouth. "It'd be a good idea if we could each take charge of a couple of horses – for mucking out and grooming at least."

"Sounds fine by me," Courtney said, "so long as I *don't* look after Fiery Lad."

"Yes, well maybe I should look after Fiery Lad." Sally raised her eyebrows. "He's not exactly the easiest of horses, is he?"

"I don't mind looking after him," Izzy jumped in quickly.

"Oh Izzy, that's really nice of you," Sally said hastily. "But I don't know if you could manage him. I mean, he's sort of a handful."

Izzy immediately bristled. She didn't know what had made her make that offer – bravado maybe – but now that Sally was looking so doubtful, Izzy felt even more determined. "Couldn't you just let me try?"

"Well, maybe," Sally paused. "Maybe he'll behave for you. Yes, why not? But if it looks as if you're having problems handling him, then I'll have to take over."

Izzy jutted out her jaw determinedly. However difficult she found Fiery Lad, there was no way she was going to show herself up and have Sally take over for her.

"You could look after Frosty as well," Sally went on, seeming not to notice Izzy's discomfort. "And then Kate could look after Sugarfoot and Tobago Bay."

"Sounds good to me," Kate answered.

"That leaves me with Seattle, Ted with Lark's Song. Oh look, don't you girls worry about the rest of it. I'll figure it out. You look beat – why don't you go on up to bed." She turned to Courtney and Megan. "Go on, you two as well."

As they stacked their dishes in the dishwasher, Kate and Izzy said good night and disappeared off up the stairs. It was only when they were in the privacy of their own room that Izzy let out a hefty sigh.

"Whew, what a day that was."

"Exhausting," Kate agreed. "And all that stuff about schedules and everything – it's going to get even busier."

Izzy shrugged, ducking quickly into the bathroom ahead of Kate. "Still, I suppose it's all part and parcel of being at a racing stables."

"I suppose so." Kate looked thoughtful as Izzy came back out. "But don't you think it's a little weird that there isn't more stable help around here?"

"Maybe they just don't work on the weekend." Izzy shrugged. She was too tired to even think about it right now, let alone talk, and as she slipped under her sheets, she felt the first delicious waves of sleep coming on. Then she sat bolt upright.

"Oh no, Kate. I've left Seattle Surprise's saddle out on the gate. Kate... Kate, can you hear me?"

But there wasn't any answer from the bathroom and it was only as Izzy listened more closely that she could hear that Kate was running a bath. Oh well, she was sure that the saddle could wait until morning. And, settling back onto her pillow, Izzy fell into a deep slumber.

The next thing Izzy knew, the sun was streaming in through the bedroom curtains and Kate was shaking her shoulder. It was morning.

"Come on, sleepyhead," Kate said. "Time to get up."

"Ugh, what time is it?" Izzy groaned.

"Six-thirty," Kate said. "You slept right through the alarm."

"Okay, I'm coming," Izzy groaned, hauling herself out of bed and into the bathroom.

Kate had already disappeared when she came back out. Izzy made her way down the stairs where Kate was sitting at the breakfast table with Courtney and Megan.

"Just in time," Megan said, passing Izzy some toast. "Eat something, then we'll head on over to the stables."

The four girls hurried through their breakfast and made their way out of the house. The ground was still wet with dew as they crossed the grass, and a yellow light was just starting to seep in across the surrounding countryside.

"Mom will already be out on the training oval by now," Megan said. "So we'll get started with the jobs. Once they're finished we can go and watch the last half hour of training if you like..."

"And have a ride?" Izzy murmured under her breath.

Kate kicked her and was quick to speak out to cover her friend. "That sounds good to me."

"Okay, let's get busy," Courtney said.

"All right," Izzy nodded. "So, where's Ted this morning?"

"Oh, he's probably in the office; he'll be out in a minute," Megan answered vaguely, and then she turned and disappeared off.

"Why did you kick me, Kate?" Izzy said once Megan was out of earshot, rubbing her sore ankle.

"Well, we should wait until we get offered a ride –

not just go demanding it," Kate said. "We are the guests here."

"All right, all right," Izzy grumbled as they walked into the barn.

Izzy went to the first stall, and led the big, bay mare into the aisle. Then she went back for Fiery Lad. While the horses were eating their breakfast, she grabbed a pitchfork and started mucking out their stalls. She didn't stop until she met Kate coming the other way – by which time she was feeling really hot and tired.

"Whew." Izzy stood upright and wiped the dirt off her forehead.

Kate grinned. "Let's go and find Courtney and Megan." She linked arms with Izzy and they walked out into the brilliant sunshine.

"All done?" Courtney called across to them.

"Yup, all done," Kate answered.

"Okay, let's go."

It wasn't far for them to walk through the paddocks to the training oval behind the stables. Sally was in the middle of the grass, her eyes fixed on a string of six racehorses. The exercise riders were crouched low in the saddles as they galloped around the outside of the track.

"The horses aren't going at full speed," Courtney explained. "They're just working out."

"Well, it still looks fast to me," Kate said.

Patiently, they waited for the horses to gallop past them, and then Courtney led them into the middle of the oval. The four girls stood a little way away from Sally so as not to disturb her.

"Have you spotted Seattle?" Courtney pointed out

36

the gray mare at the head of the string.

"How could we miss her," Kate murmured, gazing across the grass.

The gray horse really did look magnificent. Her muscled hindquarters seemed to propel her forward at such a speed. Her delicate legs were little more than a blur as she stretched out the string of horses.

"She looks great," Izzy said as Seattle Surprise's exercise rider fed her the reins and they swung around the turn.

"Yeah, she sure does, doesn't she?" Courtney said thoughtfully.

"Will we be able to go and watch her race?" Izzy asked excitedly as the training came to an end.

"I don't see why not." Courtney answered as they turned away and made their way through the paddocks. "The racetrack's only fifty miles away from here."

"Great!" Izzy said excitedly, walking through the gate. As they walked into the middle of the yard, they were surprised to see the stable manager ahead of them, holding a saddle. It looked as though he was waiting for someone and his face was thunderous.

"I don't suppose you girls know anything about this, do you?" Ted spoke quickly and sharply. "It was left out last night."

Izzy felt her heart beat faster and her face flush, but nobody said anything.

Megan hesitated. "Maybe one of the exercise riders left it out yesterday morning."

"But you girls were cleaning tack after that," Ted went on accusingly.

"Well, none of us left it out," Courtney said

37

defensively. "We'd tell you if we did."

Izzy swallowed hard. She'd forgotten all about that saddle. More than anything she'd have liked the ground to have swallowed her up. She wished she could just walk away without saying a word, but she had to own up.

"Um, look, I think it might be my fault," she said, fidgeting with her hair. "I left it on the gate... I was hurrying... I meant to go back for it but-"

"You just left it on the gate?" Ted thundered. "How could you have been so irresponsible? Don't you know how much these saddles cost?"

"It's all right, Ted." Sally called from where she was walking up the path. She came up behind the stable manager and laid a comforting hand on his arm. Ted looked as though he was about to explode. "I'll deal with this."

It didn't alter the annoyed look on Ted's face, but at least it had stopped him from shouting.

Sally put her arm around Izzy's shoulder. "Look, we do have strict rules about putting tack back where it came from, but how were you to know that?"

Izzy nodded. Ted had made her feel really small, and she was close to tears. "I didn't do it on purpose," she said.

"I'm sure you didn't," Sally said kindly. "And Ted didn't mean what he said. It's just that he takes a lot of pride in running the yard and he's under a lot of stress at the moment – as we all are. Now come on, let's put it behind us and go enjoy ourselves."

6

SURPRISE VISITORS

Izzy tried as best she could to follow Sally's advice that afternoon. It wasn't hard enjoying herself around the horses, but every time she saw Ted she was reminded of how horrible he'd been, and that put a damper on everything. The twins weren't as friendly as they'd been that first night either, but then she hadn't seen that much of them as they'd all been so busy. It was only when it was the same the next day and the one after, that Kate and Izzy started to feel a little more disgruntled. They were supposed to be guests at Graytops, but they were beginning to feel more like hired hands!

On Wednesday morning, Izzy was having a particularly difficult time, trying to groom Fiery Lad when Kate poked her head over the stable door.

"Need any help?"

"No, I'm fine," Izzy said, looking anything but

fine. "I could do with a ride, but apart from that..."

"Me too." Kate looked at her best friend. "You know, I can't understand why you were so determined to look after that horse." Kate changed the subject. "Sugarfoot's lovely – a complete dream."

"Yes, well you would say that," Izzy huffed.

"Look Izzy," Kate said. "Why don't you just give in. Tell Sally that Fiery Lad's acting up and get a nicer horse to look after."

"No way," Izzy said determinedly. "I can handle him."

"But clearly you can't," Kate said. "Look at you – you've been in here for an hour, trying to pick his feet out."

"I'll be all right." Izzy flared up. "If only they could get some help around here, things would be better. We need someone we can ask advice, but Ted's so unfriendly. And where do you think all the stable hands are? What do you think Sally does when the girls are at school?"

"Dunno," Kate said thoughtfully. "I was thinking about that myself, but it seemed kind of rude to ask. And anyway, everyone else has been working just as hard as us."

"I suppose so." Izzy nodded. "But this is their farm, and Ted's getting paid for it! Will you just keep still, Fiery Lad?" she cried, giving the horse's lead-rope a sharp tug.

"Hey, calm down, Izzy," Kate said. But it was too late. The whites of Fiery Lad's eyes flashed and he reared up on his hind legs. Izzy was totally unprepared for the stallion's reaction. She turned as white as a sheet as the horse reared up again and again, whinnying loudly. She didn't know what to do, but one thing was for sure – she didn't want Ted to hear this.

"Get out of there, Izzy," Kate said, trying to stay calm.

"All right, all right." Izzy didn't know what to do as the panic-stricken horse thrashed around in the box.

"Hush, ssshh boy," she crooned.

"We should get help," Kate said.

"No, wait a moment," Izzy cried. "He'll be all right in a second."

But Fiery Lad's frenzy wasn't abating and in spite of her words, Izzy was starting to get scared. Then she heard the sound of footsteps at the end of the barn. She turned around, her heart in her mouth.

There, at the doorway, stood a sleek, blonde-haired girl. Without stopping, the girl came rushing down the aisle, drew back the bolt on Fiery Lad's door and swooped into his stall.

Izzy and Kate stood, amazed, as she calmed the panicking horse before their eyes. Gradually his lashings became less frantic until finally the girl stood, cradling his nose in her hand.

"Take it easy, boy," the girl murmured gently. "You'll be all right now."

"Wow! That was amazing," Izzy said, full of awe. "How... how did you manage that?" Izzy opened her mouth like a goldfish and closed it again.

"Just a trick of the trade," the girl smiled.

Izzy and Kate stood there, looking at the girl. She could only be a few years older than them, but she'd handled that horse like a professional.

"Paula! Paula! Where did you go?" A voice called out from the end of the aisle.

"Fiery Lad should be all right now." The girl smiled as she drew back the bolt to the horse's stall. "I'll catch you two later." And as quickly as the girl had appeared, she disappeared.

Izzy looked at Kate, and back again at Fiery Lad. "So who do you think she was?"

"Dunno," Kate said. "But she calmed him all right."

"Yes, she did, didn't she?" Izzy lifted up Fiery Lad's foot and scraped a stone out of his shoe. "And you know, she's the first visitor we've seen at the farm since we got here. Where do you think she came from?"

"Dunno," Kate mused, looking up as she heard footsteps at the end of the barn again.

"Uh oh, I'm going to be in trouble if that girl's told Sally." Izzy raised her eyebrows and looked down the aisle toward a group, some distance away.

"Hi Izzy... Kate," Sally smiled, coming up to join them. "Let me introduce you to our vet, Dr. Doyle, and his assistant, Paula." Sally indicated the man and the blonde girl they'd just met, standing behind her. "Dr. Doyle's also the course veterinarian at Clevedon Park Racetrack, so he's pretty important. This is Kate and Izzy – they've come in from Virginia on vacation."

"Well, hi there," the vet said. "So what do you think about all these horses? He can be quite a handful, that one." He indicated Fiery Lad.

"Izzy's doing an amazing job." Sally stepped in quickly. Izzy breathed a sigh of relief. The girl – Paula

– clearly hadn't told them what had happened. Izzy shot her a grateful look.

"Izzy seems to have gotten the hang of him completely," Sally went on.

"Er, well, I don't know about that." Izzy was tongue-tied. It would have been so easy for Paula to have stepped in at that point and told them what had just happened, but she didn't say a word.

"Anyway, come on, Eric." Sally turned back to the vet. "Let's go and take a look at the yearlings." And with that, they moved out of the barn, leaving Paula behind.

"Thanks for not saying anything," Izzy said.

"There wasn't anything to say," the girl smiled.

"Well, you were amazing with Fiery Lad anyway," Izzy said admiringly. "Where did you learn to be able to manage horses like that?"

"From my Dad, I guess – he's been working with racehorses all his life. It must be in my genes," Paula laughed. "Here, let me help you with that." She picked up a broom and started to sweep.

Izzy smiled.

"So when did you two get here?" Paula went on as she helped them put their stuff away.

"Saturday," Izzy answered. "So we're quite new to the world of racehorses."

"I'm a little new to Graytops myself," Paula answered. "I've only been working for Dr. Doyle for a few months – my home's back in New York State."

"Oh, I see," Izzy nodded. The girl looked really sophisticated, but underneath she seemed as unsure of herself as they were. "So is this a summer job

43

then?"

"Yeah, something like that," Paula said. "I had planned to go to veterinary college – only my folks couldn't afford the fees. This is the next best thing."

"Oh, I see." Suddenly Izzy and Kate felt embarrassed – whether it was the talk of money, or the fact that Paula had taken them so easily into her confidence, they didn't know.

"Anyway, Dr. Doyle's been really good to me," Paula went on. "And you never know what might come of-"

She seemed about to say more, but voices at the end of the aisle pulled her up short. Izzy and Kate spun around to see Courtney rushing toward them.

"Are you guys finished in there?" Courtney called breathlessly, then she noticed Paula. "Oh, so you're here."

Izzy looked up, surprised. Was she mistaken? Or was there a very definite change in Courtney's voice when she spoke to Paula? It was unfriendly... icy even. If there was, Paula didn't seem to have noticed it.

"Oh hi, Courtney," she said. "Dr. Doyle's with your mom, so I just thought I'd take the time to meet your new friends. How's it going out here, anyway?"

"Oh you know, not too bad." Courtney was short and Izzy was relieved when she heard the sound of Megan's voice at the other end of the barn.

"Where's Dr. Doyle?" Megan squealed, rushing in. "Don't tell me I've missed him. I wanted to ask him something."

"No, you haven't missed him," Courtney sighed

and raised her eyebrows. "He's with Mom in the paddocks. Let's go over there. You coming?" She turned to Izzy and Kate.

"We'll just finish up here and then we'll be right with you," Izzy answered.

Courtney nodded and disappeared off, with Megan following not far behind.

"Wow, they're certainly a lively pair, aren't they?" Paula raised her eyebrows.

"Yes, they are," Izzy said, feeling slightly awkward at how their friends had behaved. "Do I get the impression you don't like them much?"

"I think it's more a case of them not liking me." Paula shrugged. "They've been really strange with me since I got here – well, ever since the incident with Seattle really."

"What incident with Seattle?" Izzy looked puzzled.

"Oh, it was nothing," Paula said. "But – oh you might as well know the truth. It was one afternoon – well, it looked to me as though Seattle was colicking so I called Sally over to take a look." Paula looked nonchalant, but Izzy was full of admiration. It wasn't so long ago that her own horse had nearly died of colic because she hadn't been quick enough to recognize the symptoms.

"Anyway," Paula shrugged, "Courtney and Megan didn't like it at all – and they sure didn't like the praise I got after it. You'd have thought they'd be happy that I'd saved their horse, but I think they thought I was interfering."

"How silly," Izzy said. "Surely it doesn't matter who saved the horse – the important thing is that she was saved."

"Well, that's what I thought," Paula went on. "Anyway, don't let it affect your stay here – I'm sure Courtney and Megan are really nice underneath it all." She looked about to say more, but then seemed to change her mind. "Hey, would you two be interested in going to the movies sometime? It would be nice to make a couple of friends around here."

"Well, ah, yes, that would be great." Izzy looked uncertain. They were here at Graytops as Megan and Courtney's guests – it wouldn't look very good if they made friends with someone the twins didn't like. And then Izzy felt bad. Paula had been so nice, so she smiled warmly at her.

"Great, so I take it that's a 'yes' then?" Paula looked grateful.

"Definitely." Kate stepped in.

"Okay, well, I guess I'd better be off to find Dr. Doyle. I'll catch you two later." And with that, she was gone.

"See you," Kate called out after Paula's departing figure.

"Yes, bye." Izzy turned around to look at Kate. "So what do you make of all that?"

"Dunno," Kate shrugged. "But she did seem really nice."

"Hmm, she did, didn't she?" Izzy said. "So do you think we should go out with her?"

"I don't see why not," Kate said. "We might want a change of scenery from the farm some time and she's certainly right about Courtney and Megan acting a little funny – perhaps they'd like a break from us too."

"You could be right." Izzy frowned as she thought

about it. It hadn't really crossed her mind until that point, but Courtney and Megan were supposed to be their new friends, yet they hadn't really made much of an effort at all.

7

OLD FRIENDS

"Whew, I'm drained." Kate stood upright, leaning on her broom. She was feeling tired and fed up.

"You can say that again." Izzy looked out the barn door, across the yard.

Another day had passed – another day of running around, wheeling barrows of straw, filling water-buckets, sweeping... in fact, it was all that they'd done for the five days they'd been at Graytops! At that moment, Izzy would have given almost anything to be a horse, standing outside in the shade of the trees.

"I'd love a swim," Kate said. "I thought they'd have a pool here."

"Yes, so did I." Izzy nodded. "It's certainly hot enough for one. Do you think we'll get to go out for a ride this afternoon?"

"I don't know." Kate shrugged. "They haven't

asked us yet."

"I know, it's annoying, isn't it?" Izzy said, working herself up. "Anyone would think we were being paid to work the amount of time we're putting in."

"You don't think we could have misunderstood about it being a vacation, do you?" Kate said.

"No," Izzy said. "Definitely not. It was a prize, and you wouldn't expect a prize to be just work, would you? And besides, think of all the riding that Megan and Courtney talked about in their letters. No, something doesn't add up here," Izzy mused. "And you know, I think we should say something." As Izzy stood there, with a determined look on her face, the twins approached from the aisle.

"Hi Izzy, hi Kate," Courtney smiled and Izzy softened. "Whew, it's been hard work today, hasn't it?"

"You can say that again," Kate laughed.

"Look," Megan started. "We're sorry you haven't had a chance to go out for a ride yet. We thought we might go for a long trail ride tomorrow. How about it? We could leave in the morning, take a picnic lunch and ride up into the hills."

"Oh, well yes, that sounds great." Izzy felt instantly placated. A day's ride in the hills would compensate for all the hard work – well, nearly...

*

49

As Friday morning dawned, Izzy was rudely jolted awake by the sound of the alarm clock ringing around the room. She thumped the button down with a *thwack* and leaped out of bed. As the sun streamed under the bedroom curtains, she stretched out her arms. At first she couldn't think why she had such a good feeling about today, and then she remembered. Of course!

Izzy drew back the curtains. "Come on, Kate," she cried. "We're riding this morning!"

"I can't wait!" Kate sat up, leaning on her elbows.

The two girls dressed in double-quick time and hurried down the stairs.

"I guess Courtney and Megan must have gone across to the stables ahead of us," she said, looking around her at the empty kitchen. "Do you reckon they're getting Prince and Garnet tacked up?"

"Fat chance of that," Kate giggled, picking up her mug of hot chocolate and sitting down at the breakfast table. "I've made one for you." She pointed back to the cup on the kitchen counter.

Izzy sipped her drink and put it down. Then she turned back to her friend. "Come on then, let's go."

Izzy and Kate were in so much of a hurry to get across to the yard that they didn't even notice that Sally's car wasn't in its usual spot that morning. As they turned the corner to the stables, it was all very quiet.

"They're probably in one of the barns," Izzy said. "Courtney! Megan! We're here."

"Strange," Kate said, looking up and down the aisle. "There doesn't seem to be anyone around."

As they came out into the yard, the bright sunlight dazzled them.

50

"Oh, it's you." Ted's voice called across to them. "I wondered when you two might make it out here."

Izzy didn't know whether it was the sight of the stable manager, or just his tone of voice, but something started to make her feel mad.

"Are we late for something?" she asked indignantly.

"Well no, not exactly late, but the horses do need to be taken out to the paddocks," Ted replied.

"So where are Courtney and Megan then?" Kate asked. "We're supposed to be going out for a ride with them."

"Yes, well you'll have to wait for that," Ted said. "The girls have had to go out with Sally."

"Go out?" Izzy looked furious. "Where have they gone out to?"

"That's nothing to do with you," Ted answered gruffly. "I'm supposed to let you know that they'll be back by three."

"Three!" Kate gasped. "So what do we do until then?"

Ted shrugged. "Well, as I said – those horses need to be taken out and then there's the mucking out and all of the water buckets need to be filled." And with that, he was gone.

"Of all the-" Izzy was fuming. "They haven't even had the decency to leave us a note, and to top it all, they've left us with all the work! Well, I'm simply not doing it! There is something really strange going on at this place!"

"Oh come on, Izzy," Kate said. "Ted's obviously under a huge amount of pressure and there's no one else around."

51

"Well, he can do it himself," Izzy said, standing with her hands on her hips.

"The horses will be the ones to suffer," Kate reminded her.

"I don't care," Izzy frowned. But she did care, and as she stood there, her face set in a frown, she knew she would give in. She took a deep breath. "I suppose you're right – we *have* to help. It's just that everything's so awful out here."

"I know, I feel exactly the same as you," Kate's voice caught. "I can't help comparing everything to how it would be at Sandy Lane – all of the riding we'd be doing if we were back there."

"Yes, I know." Izzy rubbed her eyes to fight back the tears. And then she turned to Kate. "You know, I've got an idea – something we could do that might cheer us up. What time is it?"

"8 o'clock," Kate said, looking puzzled.

"That's 9 o'clock in Virginia," Izzy said slowly. "Everyone will be at Sandy Lane. Let's call them – give them a surprise. We can find out how they did at Colcott last weekend. What do you say?"

"Well, I don't know." Kate was hesitant. "It's expensive to call home, and the horses do need our help."

"Five minutes won't hurt," Izzy pleaded. "That'll be all it'll take, and then we can come back and start mucking out. And as for the cost – well, we can always pay Sally back. Mom gave me some money, and we haven't even had a chance to spend anything yet."

"Okay," Kate said slowly. "Okay, you've convinced me."

"Come on then," Izzy said.

And so, the two girls dashed out of the barn, across the gravel and up the steps of the house. Quickly, they pushed back the screen door and hurried through the kitchen, down the hallway to the study. Without a second thought, Izzy picked up the receiver.

"Here goes," Izzy said, dialing the number. Impatiently, she waited as the ring tone sounded. "Come on, there must be someone around!"

And then someone started speaking.

"Hello, Sandy Lane Stables..."

"Who's that?" Izzy said excitedly.

"Rosie..." a mystified voice came from the other end.

"Rosie, it's Izzy – Izzy and Kate. How are you? How's everything going at Sandy Lane?"

Kate craned her neck over the receiver to try and listen in.

"Everything's great." Rosie's voice came. "The horses are great; the weather's great; I don't know where to start."

"Start with Midnight," Izzy cried impatiently.

"Well, he's doing wonderfully." Rosie's voice came again. "Missing you, of course."

"And how did you all do at Colcott?" Izzy said excitedly.

"Oh, Jess came second in the Tack-and-Turnout, and Alex came third in the Working Hunter, and the new girl – Clare Testar – she won the Under 13.2 Hands. Oh and then Midnight and I-"

"Yes," Izzy said impatiently.

"We won. We won the Open Jumping!" Rosie sounded pleased, but a little embarrassed.

"You won, Rosie? But that's great," Izzy cried.

Her heart wrenched. It was great that Rosie had won, but if she had been back home, she might have won on Midnight herself. Almost immediately she felt bad for having such mean thoughts.

"So how's it all going out there?" Rosie's voice interrupted her thoughts. "Don't tell me you're riding real racehorses – it'll only make me sick with envy. And what's the weather like? Is it really hot?"

"Well yes it is," Izzy said tentatively, not knowing what to say. "But Graytops is different than a riding stable."

"I'm sure it is," Rosie said. "I bet you're having an amazing time."

"Well yes, of course we are," Izzy said, trying to muster up some enthusiasm. Suddenly, this phone call seemed all wrong. She couldn't tell Rosie they were having a lousy time. What would everyone say? What would Sarah think? She took a deep breath.

"So I guess you won't be wanting to come home now!" Rosie exclaimed.

"No, definitely not," Izzy laughed nervously.

"Look Izzy, I don't mean to be rude." Rosie's voice came again. "But I'm going to have to cut you short. The 1 o'clock hack's just come in and the yard's in absolute chaos."

"Of course," Izzy said with relief. "We've got to go ourselves."

"Another racehorse waiting?" Rosie giggled.

"Hmm, something like that," Izzy said. "Okay, bye... yes, see you in a couple of weeks."

And that was the end of the conversation. Kate looked glum as Izzy put down the receiver.

"Well, that's that then," Izzy said. "Everyone

expects us to be having such a wonderful time out here – it's really embarrassing to think that we're not."

"I know," Kate said gloomily. "But we shouldn't be embarrassed. It's not our fault."

"No, it's not," Izzy said, thinking hard. "And you know, I think we should have a talk with Courtney and Megan when they get back. There's nothing to stop us from changing our flights and going home early."

"No, I don't suppose there is," Kate agreed. "But we really should give Courtney and Megan a chance to explain first."

"Of course we should," Izzy said calmly. "But that's all it's going to be – a chance to explain exactly what's going on. There's something odd going on at Graytops – and I want to know what it is."

8

REVELATIONS

Izzy looked at her watch as she paced up and down the living room. "5 o'clock!" she said. "5 o'clock and they're still not back yet!"

As the 3 o'clock deadline had approached – and passed – Izzy and Kate had found themselves becoming more and more frustrated.

"What's that?" Kate listened hard. If she wasn't mistaken, there was the sound of wheels on gravel. And now, as she listened more closely, she could definitely hear car doors slamming. Kate jumped to her feet and looked out of the window. Sally's car had pulled up in the driveway and now Courtney and Megan were running up the driveway.

"They're back," Kate said.

"Great." Izzy plopped herself down in the nearest armchair and folded her arms.

"Izzy! Kate! Where are you?" Courtney and

Megan's voices rang out through the house.

"Don't answer," Izzy hissed. "Let them find us."

"All right," Kate said, trying to look nonchalant as she flipped through a horse magazine.

"Oh, there you are." Courtney said breathlessly as her face appeared around the doorway. "Ready for a ride?"

"We *were*." Izzy sat, looking stony-faced.

"Yes, look, we're really sorry, but something very important came up," Courtney apologized. "Still, we can go out now, can't we?"

"It's a little late for that, isn't it?" Izzy said moodily.

"Don't be silly," Megan said. "The sun will still be up for a few more hours."

"Unless you don't want to." Courtney raised her eyebrows.

"Want to? What do you think we've been wanting to do all week?" Izzy exploded. "You've been treating us like hired hands, and we're not even getting paid for it! All we seem to do is muck out, groom horses and do all the work that stable hands normally do! We're having a terrible time – such a terrible time that we wish we'd never come. In fact, we're going to change our flights and go home early!"

"Oh no, don't do that." Courtney said hastily. "I know that it hasn't been the greatest here. Dad wanted us to cancel your trip, but Mom said that we couldn't."

"Dad?" Izzy was intrigued. This was the first time the twins had mentioned their father.

"Yes – Dad." Courtney looked puzzled.

"So why didn't he cancel our trip?" Kate said. "It would have been the best thing all around if your parents are having problems with their marriage."

"Problems with their marriage?" Courtney looked shocked. "They're not having problems with their marriage."

"Then where *is* your father?" Izzy blurted out before she had a chance to think how it sounded.

"Well, uh... he had to move out," Courtney said vaguely. "But it's not because of Mom. Did you really think that?"

"If only you would tell us what's going on, we might be able to understand," Kate said, feeling frustrated.

"But Mom and Dad don't want us to talk about it," Megan hesitated, looking nervously at Courtney.

"But maybe the circumstances have changed now, Megan," Courtney softened. "We owe it to Izzy and Kate to tell them just what's been going on – especially if we want to get them to stay."

"Okay, well, let's sit down and talk," Megan said slowly.

Kate and Izzy looked uncertain, but they did as they were told and sat down on the sofa.

"Well." Courtney took a deep breath. "We'll have to go back a few months for you to understand what's happening now."

"Things were going really well at the farm back then," Megan joined in. "We were on a real winning streak. It's taken a while for Dad to get his reputation off the ground, but more and more people were sending their horses to him..."

"But then Sugarfoot was drug-tested after a big race," Courtney stepped in. "And he tested positive – an antihistamine was found in his system!"

Izzy gasped. "At home, a horse isn't allowed to

race with any kind of drug in its system. It might act as a stimulant and give the horse an unfair advantage."

"Well exactly," Courtney said seriously. "It's the same in Kentucky."

"Dad was called before the track stewards and asked to explain himself," Megan said. "But of course he didn't know what to say. Sugarfoot hadn't been on any sort of prescription so he didn't know how the antihistamine could have gotten into her system. Dad didn't have a previous record, and the drug was only a class five-"

"That's the lowest type of drug offense," Courtney stepped in to explain.

Megan nodded and continued. "So the stewards decided they wouldn't suspend him – they only gave him a fine. But Sugarfoot was still disqualified and placed last – the owner lost the whole purse."

"Dad was lucky it was only a class five drug," Courtney said. "A class one drug carries a $5,000 fine and up to a five year suspension for the trainer."

"I don't know what to say." Izzy looked shocked. "How on earth could the antihistamine have gotten there?"

"Well, that's what we were all asking ourselves," Megan said, looking at her sister.

"Dad felt that the only thing he could do was to get rid of all the casual staff," Courtney went on.

"So is that why you have so little stable help here?" Izzy asked, everything suddenly falling into place.

"Yeah, there were a lot of really unhappy people, but Dad had to do it," Megan said. "As it turned out, it was all for nothing as it happened again a month later – this time with Tobago Bay."

Izzy gasped.

"But this time it was so much worse," Megan said. "You see this time it was a class three drug called benzocaine."

"MEGAN!" Courtney hissed furiously. "You heard what Dad said – he didn't want any of us mentioning the name of the drug to anyone."

Megan looked scared. "Don't tell Dad I said anything – he'll be furious with me."

"Why didn't he want anyone mentioning the name of the drug?" Izzy looked puzzled.

"I don't know really," Megan shrugged. "I guess he thought it might help in some way."

"Still," Izzy said. "We're not exactly going to go telling anyone, are we? So what happened next?"

"Well," Courtney paused. "Dad got a $1,500 fine and a three month suspension – and that's why he's not at the farm right now."

Izzy let out a low whistle.

"Mom's taken over as temporary trainer in his place," Megan explained hurriedly. "You can guess that it's really hard for her – she really misses Dad."

"But this is so unfair," Kate said. "If your father knows nothing about the drugs, why should he have to leave his home?"

"You've got to think how it looks to the stewards though," Courtney answered sensibly. "And a trainer *is* the one who's responsible for the condition of his horses, which includes making sure that no one has a chance to give a horse an illegal drug."

"So is this why you've got the security guard? To protect the horses?" Izzy said.

"Exactly," Courtney answered. "A lot of farms have

60

security guards, but we've never felt the need for one before. I'm sorry I acted so weird when you mentioned him – it's just that it took me a little by surprise that you knew about him. You see Mom wants him to stay out of sight. If anyone unusual turns up at the farm she wants to be able to catch them."

"Yes, of course," Izzy said.

"We just can't risk it happening again," Megan joined in. "We've already had owners take their horses away. In fact, that was why we couldn't come to meet you at the airport."

"The trailer!" Izzy exclaimed, remembering the horse they'd seen being loaded the night they'd arrived; and she'd thought that had just been part and parcel of a racing stables.

"You'd have thought that our owners would have given Dad the benefit of the doubt," Megan said angrily. "But drugs are a dirty word in the racing business. And now, people have even started saying that all the other Graytops' horses must have won while they were on drugs too – designer drugs that couldn't be detected in the tests."

"But that's crazy," Kate cried.

"Of course it's crazy," Megan agreed. "But think how it looks. And what if it happens again? Seattle Surprise runs in her big race next week. It would be the end for Graytops if she tested positive – we'd lose even more owners. We'd have to sell the farm and we've lived here all our lives – there's always been a member of the Bryant family at Graytops for as long as anyone can remember. It's too awful to consider."

"All right, all right, Megan," Courtney said, laying

a steadying hand on her sister's shoulder. "It's not going to come to that. Seattle will be fine when she runs."

"But what if she isn't?" Megan sobbed. "What happens then?"

"We just can't think like that," Courtney said firmly. Then she turned to Kate and Izzy. "Look, I'm really sorry we weren't here for your ride this morning. We had to go with Mom to see the stewards at Clevedon Park to smooth things over – she didn't want to go by herself."

"Yes, I understand," Izzy murmured. "And what did the stewards say?"

"Well, they're letting us run Seattle next week," Courtney said. "So that's something."

"Look, this is a lot for you to take in." Megan pulled herself together. "But the most important thing is for you to decide whether you want to stay or not. If you think it's going to be too much for you, I'm sure you'll be able to change your tickets."

"We'd love you to stay," Courtney joined in. "We don't know how we'd have managed without all your help. And of course we'd try and make sure you got to do tons of riding..."

"Look," Megan said. "Why don't you and Kate take Prince and Garnet out now? You could talk it over and make a decision."

"That sounds like a good idea," Izzy said, looking at Kate, who nodded in agreement.

A ride was exactly what they needed, but as for talking it all through and making a decision – well, they wouldn't have to do that. As soon as Megan had uttered her sentence about it being too much for them, she had unwittingly laid down a challenge, and one that Izzy and Kate weren't going to refuse. Besides, the Bryants needed all the help they could get – how else could they look after all the horses?

9

POINTING THE FINGER

Izzy swung up into the saddle and gathered up the reins to Garnet's bridle. Briefly she bent down to pat his chestnut neck.

"This feels good." She twisted around to call back to Kate. "I'd almost forgotten what it felt like to sit on a horse."

"Yeah, me too." Kate laughed as she clucked Prince on down the grassy lanes between the paddocks.

The sun was low in the sky by now, casting the farm in a soft golden light, and as the two girls wound their way through the countryside, they left the farm far behind them.

"So, what do you make of it all, Izzy?" Kate said, pushing Prince on into a trot through a line of lime trees.

"Well, I don't really know," Izzy answered breathlessly. "I mean... I never imagined anything like this could be going on. No wonder everyone's been so uptight. I feel awful about making such a fuss about our riding when they've had so much to worry about."

"You can say that again," Kate said, rising to the steady rhythm of Prince's trot. "But you know, Izzy, this is going to sound really bad, but I've got to say it."

"Go on then." Izzy looked across and drew Garnet to a walk.

"Tell me if you think I'm jumping to silly conclusions." Kate fiddled nervously with the reins. "But what if the Bryants really have been doping their own horses? I don't want to be staying with dishonest trainers."

"No." Izzy bent down to pat Garnet's neck. "Neither do I, but I don't think they would have done something like that. I know that they look like the obvious choice, but it doesn't make any sense – why would they drug their own horses when they'd know the horses would only get drug-tested at the end of the race? They'd know that they couldn't get away with it."

"That's true." Kate felt relieved. "And Sarah's known the Bryants for years – surely she wouldn't be friends with people who were capable of something like doping."

"No." Izzy looked thoughtful. "I don't think she would. I think we've got to look somewhere else for an answer, and you know, I've had a thought – do you remember back at Sandy Lane when Rosie got caught up in that doping scandal?"

"Yes, of course I do," Kate said.

The incident Izzy was referring to had been a

couple of years back. Rosie had befriended a local stable boy who'd been accused of trying to dope a racehorse – only in the end, it had turned out to be a rival trainer who was responsible.

"Yes, I see exactly where you're coming from." Kate looked excited. "It could be a rival trainer involved here too, couldn't it?"

Izzy nodded. "I wonder who trained the horses that came in second in each race. We ought to ask Courtney and Megan about that – it might be connected."

"I take it you don't think we should go back home then?" Kate raised her eyebrows.

"Definitely not." Izzy gritted her teeth, her eyes fixed determinedly on the grass track ahead. "You heard what Courtney said – we'll get to ride a lot more now and besides, we might be able to help them get to the bottom of it."

"Oh Izzy," Kate groaned as she gathered up Garnet's reins. "I don't think we should get involved in all that. Look, we've done enough talking for one day, let's gallop!"

*

Izzy and Kate clattered into the stable yard in high spirits. Of course what had happened at Graytops was bad news, but at least now that they knew what was going on they could understand why everyone had been behaving so strangely.

"Come on," Izzy said, jumping down from Prince's saddle and leading the little pony off. "Let's get these ponies rubbed down and go find Courtney and Megan."

Izzy and Kate led the ponies off into the barn. Although they were anxious to go and find their friends, they were careful not to skimp on their tasks. By the time they had finished, Garnet and Prince's coats shone like burnished mahogany.

As Izzy and Kate headed across the grass and climbed the stairs to the porch that evening, the dusk was already starting to creep in.

"Courtney... Megan," Kate called, pushing back the front door and walking down the hallway.

"Up here," a voice called from upstairs. Izzy and Kate climbed the stairs and pushed back the door to Courtney's bedroom.

"We were just listening to some music," Megan said.

"Is your mom around?" Kate whispered. "Can we talk?"

"Yes, we can talk. She's on the phone with Dad in the study," Courtney said. "She knows that you know everything now."

"And did she mind?" Izzy said.

"A little at first – she was kind of worried about you being dragged into it all," Megan said. "But then I think she realized we couldn't keep it a secret from you any longer."

"So, what have you decided?" Courtney asked. "Are you staying?"

"Of course we're staying!" Kate answered.

"Great!" Courtney's face lit up.

"And we've had an idea," Izzy stepped in. "An idea about who could be behind all of this. You see, we've come across something like this before back in Virginia."

"There was a racehorse at Sandy Lane that was being doped," Kate joined in excitedly. "It caused such a big stir at Sandy Lane when everyone found out how deeply Rosie was involved."

"Rosie's our friend," Izzy explained, and then, seeing the horrified looks on Courtney and Megan's faces, she jumped in quickly to explain. "Oh no, she wasn't involved like that. She was only trying to help. You see she was involved with this stable boy. He was on the run – accused of having doped a horse. Only, it turned out that it wasn't him at all-"

"It was a rival trainer," Kate interrupted.

Izzy and Kate paused and looked across to see if they could read anything in Courtney and Megan's faces.

"And you think the same thing might be happening here?" Courtney said slowly.

"Well yes," Izzy said. "What about the trainer of the horses that came in second?"

"Actually, we've been down this road before," Megan said gloomily. "And coincidentally they were trained by the same man."

"Well that's it then," Izzy cried out excitedly.

"I'm afraid it's not," Courtney said firmly. "You see the trainer – Joe Hagan – is a friend of our family's. He wouldn't do anything to hurt Dad."

"But how do you know that?" Izzy said, putting her thinking cap on. "I mean, what if he was harboring a secret grudge? Or had money troubles – anything like that might make him act in a way that was out of character." She looked at Courtney and Megan, expecting them to look pleased with her theory, but neither of them looked very pleased.

"It just isn't possible," Courtney said.

"It was only an idea." Izzy suddenly wished she hadn't mentioned it.

"Well, Joe just isn't like that," Megan jumped in quickly.

"All right, so maybe it's someone else you know," Kate stepped in, realizing that if she didn't mediate immediately, they'd be in the middle of a full-scale argument. "I don't think Izzy meant it was definitely him – it was just a thought."

"Well, Joe hasn't been to Graytops in ages," Courtney said triumphantly. "So it couldn't be him."

"Oh hmm..." Izzy looked disappointed.

"I don't even know why we're talking like this," Courtney said angrily. "Seattle's going to be just fine when she races."

"Yes, of course she is," Kate said.

"Look, Courtney didn't mean to be defensive," Megan said placatingly. "She's just upset. Let's try and forget about this for now, all right?"

And that, it seemed, was the end of the conversation. Courtney's words had been firm and self-assured, and if Izzy hadn't seen the worried look in her eyes, she would almost have believed her about Seattle's race. But it just wasn't true – no one knew for sure that everything would be all right when Seattle ran, and now all they could do was just sit back and wait.

10

AN UNUSUAL OFFER

"They should be trying to figure out who could be behind all this, not just waiting for Seattle's race," Izzy said, leaning over the top of Garnet's stall. "It's all so passive."

"I agree," Kate nodded.

The weekend had passed quickly – quicker than either Kate or Izzy could have imagined, given the circumstances.

"But Courtney and Megan seem so unresponsive to any ideas on who it could be," Izzy moaned. "You heard how they reacted when we suggested it could be Joe Hagan – they completely disregarded the possibility."

"Yes, but he is a friend of their father's," Kate said fairly. "Think how we'd feel if they accused one of our Sandy Lane friends of something awful."

"I guess," Izzy answered. "But I just can't believe

70

how uptight they're being."

"But then wouldn't you be if something as important as this was at stake?" Kate said. "I mean, think of the thing that matters most to you in the world."

"Thinking," Izzy said, conjuring up an image in her mind.

"Don't tell me," Kate laughed. "It doesn't have a silky black neck and big black eyes, does it?"

"You guessed it," Izzy laughed.

"Well," Kate went on. "Just imagine if Midnight was going to be taken away from you."

"Never," Izzy said fiercely.

"Exactly," Kate said. "It didn't take much to get a reaction out of you, did it? So we should try to understand how Courtney and Megan are feeling, and if they're so certain that Joe isn't involved, then we should just drop the subject."

"Yes, maybe," Izzy said, though she didn't look entirely convinced. "It's just that I can't get it out of my head, and I can't bear just sitting around doing nothing."

"It doesn't look like you're sitting around doing nothing to me," a voice came from the end of the barn.

Izzy and Kate spun around. "Paula!" They smiled, pleased to see the vet's assistant. She hadn't been back to Graytops since last week and it was nice to see a friendly face. "What are you doing here?"

"Oh, Dr. Doyle's come to check on Seattle Surprise, so I thought I'd come and see how you two were doing. Are you by yourselves?"

Kate nodded. "Courtney and Megan have gone

out for a ride."

"What – and left you to do all of the hard work?" Paula laughed.

"Well, not exactly." Izzy jumped to the twins' defense. She didn't know exactly why, but since they had revealed so much about what was going on, she felt rather protective of them.

"We've done tons of riding this weekend," Kate went on. "And Courtney and Megan really needed a break from the farm – they haven't had a chance to go out since we got here."

"Of course." Paula nodded. "I was only joking."

Just at that moment, the conversation was broken up as Ted appeared at the end of the barn. "I thought I could hear another voice in here."

"Only me," Paula started. But she didn't get very far. Before she could get another word out, Ted had turned on his heel and was walking back down the aisle.

"Not the friendliest guy in the world, is he?" Paula commented.

"You can say that again." Izzy was quick to join in with any criticism of Ted. "He's been a real nightmare since we got here."

Kate frowned at Izzy. It was all right to talk like that to each other, but she didn't think Sally would be too pleased if she heard they were bad-mouthing the staff.

"Well, don't worry about him. What were you two jabbering about anyway?" Paula asked. "It sounded important."

Izzy looked at Kate. She was aching to talk to someone else about everything that was going on at

Graytops, but she didn't know how much of it was public knowledge.

Izzy hesitated. "We've just found out some stuff about Graytops, that's all."

"Oh, you mean all the stuff about the doping?" Paula said.

"Well yes, exactly," Izzy said. She didn't know whether to feel relieved that she hadn't had to let the cat out of the bag, or upset that they were the only ones who hadn't known. Still, she supposed it was hardly surprising that the vet's assistant knew just what was going on.

"It's terrible, isn't it?" Paula shrugged. "Their whole business is at stake."

Izzy looked at Kate. Should they take Paula into their confidence and tell her their 'rival trainer theory'? They didn't know her all that well, but she seemed nice and perhaps she'd be able to look at it more clearly and tell them if they were barking up the wrong tree.

Kate looked at Izzy and nodded.

"Well, we had an idea," Izzy started. "You see, we came across something like this back home – at our local stables."

"A horse was being doped," Kate said. "It turned out to be a rival trainer and we thought – well, what if it was the same here?"

Paula looked thoughtful, but she didn't say anything.

"Courtney and Megan went nuts when we suggested it," Kate went on. "You see the trainer of both of the horses that came in second was a man named Joe Hagan. Courtney and Megan are adamant

73

that he couldn't be involved – they say he's a friend of their Dad's."

"I know Joe Hagan," Paula looked thoughtful, scratching her head. "His farm's not that far away from here. I've been there with Dr. Doyle. You know, I don't like him at all. He's a mean piece of work if you ask me. And if the Bryants had to close down their farm he'd probably get some of their horses. I wouldn't trust him as far as I could throw him."

"Really?" Izzy breathed, casting a quick glance at Kate. This was getting interesting.

"Yeah, really," Paula went on. "He's always arguing over our bills... says we're overcharging him. I don't know why Dr. Doyle keeps going back there. I guess it must be for the sake of the horses."

"So it looks as though Joe Hagan could be struggling financially, does it?" Izzy said.

"Well, I don't know about that," Paula said quickly. "But I don't think he's as clean as Courtney and Megan seem to think. But maybe you could do something. If you really want to help Graytops, that is."

"Of course we want to help Graytops," Izzy said immediately. "But Courtney and Megan want us to forget the whole idea."

"Well," Paula paused. "Why don't you go and check out Joe Hagan's farm yourselves? You never know what you might find – some of the drugs that were found in the horses – anything like that might give him away."

"Oh, but we couldn't go behind Courtney and Megan's backs," Izzy said quickly. "Besides, we wouldn't know how to get there."

"I could take you," Paula said, "in my car."

"You've got a car?" Izzy and Kate looked surprised.

"Well, I am seventeen, you know," Paula said.

"Still, we couldn't exactly just turn up at Joe Hagan's farm uninvited, could we?" Kate said. "What would we say? *'Excuse me, are you doping the Bryants' horses?'*"

"Of course you wouldn't say that," Paula laughed. "You wouldn't have to say anything at all if you went there at night-time. Joe Hagan doesn't lock up the stable yard, and there isn't a security guard... it would be pretty easy," Paula said, getting carried away with her ideas.

Kate looked shocked.

"Well, what do you say?" Paula said simply. "We'd only have to climb over a small wall."

"We?" Kate looked at Izzy and then back to Paula.

"Well yes, I'd come with you," Paula said.

Kate looked undecided but then she spoke out. "Look Paula, it's really nice of you to offer to help, but I don't really think we can do that. We'd be in such trouble if we were caught." She looked at Izzy, willing her to back her up, but Izzy didn't say a word.

"Oh, well, okay then." Paula looked hurt. "Maybe I could just go by myself."

"Oh no, Paula, you can't do that!" Izzy and Kate looked uncomfortable and they both felt relieved when Paula changed the subject.

"Anyway," Paula smiled. "I'd better get out to the paddocks. Dr. Doyle will be wondering what I've been up to." She turned to make her way down the aisle and then she turned back. "Hey, look, I don't suppose you would want to go to the movies sometime this week?"

"Yes," Izzy grinned. "That sounds great. What do you think, Kate?"

"Yes, great. I'm sure it would be okay with Sally," Kate answered, hoping that their enthusiasm might make up for their rather negative reaction to Paula's other suggestion.

"Then how about Wednesday?" Paula said.

"Wednesday sounds good," Izzy nodded.

"I'll come and pick you up at around seven-thirty then," Paula said.

And with that, she turned out of the barn. As soon as she was out of earshot, Kate turned to Izzy.

"You do think we did the right thing, don't you?" she said. "Turning down Paula's offer, I mean."

"I guess so." Izzy lingered over her words. "It would be so embarrassing if we were caught – how would we explain it to Sally? To Nick and Sarah? To our parents?"

"For one moment, I thought you were going to say we should go along with it," Kate chuckled.

"No, of course not," Izzy said, turning back to braid Garnet's mane. And that was the end of the conversation. Izzy was relieved when finally Kate turned back to grooming Prince. Izzy felt sure that if Kate had seen the look of disappointment on her face, Kate would have known she wasn't quite so sure about not agreeing to Paula's scheme.

11

STAKEOUT

Life settled down at Graytops to pretty much how it had been before all of the revelations. Izzy and Kate continued to do their fair share of mucking out and grooming – only they didn't mind helping out so much now that they knew it was all going to help Graytops. And anyway, they were getting to do plenty of riding too. Sally was preoccupied with Seattle's training that week so it wasn't until Wednesday afternoon that Kate and Izzy had a chance to broach the subject of their outing to the movies with Paula. It was almost time for supper and they were sitting at the kitchen table in the farmhouse, drinking glasses of cold orange juice, when finally they spoke out.

"So you see, we wouldn't be back late," Kate cajoled.

"Yes, of course you can go," Sally said. "It'll be good for you to get away from the farm, but you have to be back by ten. I don't know what time your parents allow you to stay out, but that's our curfew time."

"Thanks, Sally." Izzy turned to Kate and gave her a wink. They were never allowed out later than nine at home.

"So where are you two going?" Courtney slid into the kitchen in her socks, nibbling a carrot.

"To a movie," Kate said, "with Paula."

"With Paula?" Megan wrinkled up her nose. "Well, I'm sure you'll have fun at the movies, but I can think of other people I'd rather go with."

Izzy looked behind her where Sally was disappearing out of the kitchen. What was it with Paula and Courtney and Megan? If she didn't have it out with the twins now, then she never would.

"Um, so just what is it that you don't like about Paula?" Izzy eased in gently.

"Oh, it's nothing really," Courtney shrugged, obviously not willing to talk about it. "Nothing important anyway."

"No, come on." Izzy pushed her, starting to feel a little annoyed. "I mean, I'm interested to hear your reasoning. She's been nothing but nice to us since we got here, and it's hard for her being new around here and everything."

"Whatever you say." Courtney didn't flinch, and that riled Izzy even more. "But maybe you don't know her as well as I do."

"I'd have thought you'd be grateful to the girl who saved Seattle's life." Izzy blurted the words out.

"Izzy!" Kate stepped in quickly, aware that her friend might have overstepped the mark this time.

"No, that's all right, Kate." Courtney held up her

hand. "Just what exactly do you mean '*saved Seattle's life*'?"

"Just what I said," Izzy said, stumbling down a route from which there was no going back.

"Is that what she said?" Courtney chuckled to herself.

Izzy didn't like Courtney's tone. She didn't like it at all. "Yes, that's what she said." Izzy jutted out her jaw.

"Then she's a better liar than I thought she was," Courtney said finally.

"Come on Courtney," Megan burst out. "Don't get into this."

"Why would she lie about it?" Izzy rose to the challenge. "She recognized the symptoms, she called your mom and you didn't like it."

"Well, that's what she said." Courtney snorted. "Paula wouldn't know the symptoms of colic if they hit her in the face. *I* was the one who went and got Mom."

"It's true," Megan joined in. "Courtney saved Seattle's life."

Izzy opened her mouth to say more, and closed it again.

"Come on, Izzy." Kate stepped in to save an argument. "We ought to go and get ready."

Izzy nodded and, without another word, she followed Kate to the door. She could have kicked herself. They had been getting along so well with Courtney and Megan lately, and now she'd really gone and blown it. It was only when they were safely behind closed doors that Kate spoke.

"Well, you really know how to ruffle someone's

feathers, don't you?"

"Yes, well, she had it coming to her," Izzy muttered under her breath, feeling a little guilty. "All those sneaky little comments about Paula – and as for her saying she'd saved Seattle's life..."

"Hmm, just what do you think it is they don't like about Paula?" Kate said.

"I don't know," Izzy hesitated. "You saw how great Paula was that day with Fiery Lad."

"Yes, she was, wasn't she?" Kate said. "It does all seem a little weird that the twins don't like her, but-"

Beeeep. Izzy and Kate's conversation was interrupted by the sound of a car horn outside.

"Oh great," Izzy said, rushing over to the window. "She's already here and I'm not ready yet. Cool car..." She turned back to Kate.

"Why, what is it?" Kate said, rushing over to join her and peering out to see an old red convertible sitting outside. "Yes it is, isn't it. It's a little beaten-up, but still cool. Come on then, let's go."

The two girls bolted down the stairs, calling out their goodbyes.

"Don't forget – ten o'clock." Sally's voice followed them as they rushed down the outside steps.

"We won't," they called, sprinting across the gravel to the car.

"Hi," Paula smiled. "All set?"

*

It was just starting to get dark as Izzy, Kate and Paula came out of the movie theater that evening.

"That was fantastic," Kate said. "Absolutely fantastic – the part where Jack told them he was Emily's real father – well, I'd never have guessed it."

"It was good, wasn't it?" Paula chuckled as they walked over to the car. "Izzy... Izzy, are you okay? You've been really quiet all evening."

"Yes I'm fine." Izzy looked up. If the truth was known, she wasn't fine. She wasn't fine at all. In fact, she'd been feeling really upset since her run-in with Courtney. She had to hear Paula's slant on Seattle's colic. It was really preying on her mind.

"Paula," Izzy started.

"Yes." Paula looked puzzled.

"You remember that incident you told us about where you saved Seattle's life?" Izzy said.

"Yes," Paula hesitated.

"Well." Izzy looked embarrassed. "I had an argument with Courtney about it before we left."

"Oh what now?" Paula groaned. "I don't know, those two girls – they never give up, do they?"

"Well," Izzy started slowly. "Courtney wouldn't have it – she said that she was the one who'd saved Seattle, not you."

"Well she would, wouldn't she?" Paula raised her hands in mock disbelief. "She wouldn't give me the credit for anything. You don't believe her though, do you?"

"Well no, not exactly," Izzy said.

"Well, either you do or you don't." Paula jutted out her jaw. "I told you how weird they'd acted with me since I arrived."

"Yes, I know," Izzy said quickly. "And of course I believe you."

Seeing how upset it had made Paula was all the confirmation that Izzy needed.

"I just can't believe it," Paula went on, running her hands through her hair. "Still, I don't know why I should have expected anything different. I guess I shouldn't think about it. It'll only tick me off even more. Look..." Quickly she changed the subject. "You know what we were talking about the other day – about going to Joe Hagan's? Well, I was thinking I might go over to his farm tonight after I've dropped you off."

"Oh." Izzy and Kate didn't know what else to say.

"I hate to admit it, but I'm feeling a little chicken about it," Paula went on, laughing nervously. "I keep panicking that I'll get caught. Anyway, I'm sure I'm just being paranoid. You do think it'll be all right, don't you?" She turned and looked at Izzy.

"Well, I don't know." Izzy looked at Kate. She felt guilty – after all, they were the ones who'd made Paula think about all of this.

"It's the car that I'm worried about," Paula went on. "I can leave it outside, but what if someone finds it? If only I had a friend who could sit outside and keep watch for me – then I wouldn't feel so nervous."

"Well..." Izzy hesitated. "I suppose we could do that, couldn't we, Kate? I mean, it wouldn't exactly be trespassing, would it?"

"No, I don't suppose it would." Kate felt equally torn. She looked at her watch. "It's nine-forty now. Sally said we had to be back by ten."

"We could manage that easily!" Paula exclaimed. "Joe Hagan's farm is on the way back."

Izzy looked at Kate and grinned. "Well, okay then."

"Great," Paula smiled. "Then let's go."

Five minutes later, Izzy and Kate found themselves being driven down the highway, the wind whipping their hair. And then Paula was turning on her turn signal and they were turning off the road, and going up a steep hill.

"It's not far now," Paula said as the car rattled down a winding road. Finally, she slowed down and turned off the engine, cruising along in neutral.

"Okay then." The car ground to a halt and Paula turned to face the two girls. "Wish me luck." But she didn't move and Izzy and Kate didn't know what to say.

"Okay," Izzy said finally, snapping out of her seat belt. "I'm coming with you."

"Are you sure?" Paula held her gaze.

"Positive," Izzy answered determinedly. "You stay here with the car, Kate," she said.

"But Izzy..." Kate called plaintively.

But it was too late. Paula was already springing up the wall and now Izzy was following on behind her. Kate took a deep breath and sank back down into her seat. This was crazy... absolutely crazy.

*

"Ssshh," Paula turned and motioned to Izzy, putting a finger to her lips.

"Maybe this isn't such a good idea after all," Izzy hesitated.

"Don't worry, we're not going to get caught," Paula said firmly.

"Do they have guard dogs in here?" Izzy murmured in a frightened voice. Now that she was inside, she didn't feel nearly so bold.

"No, nothing like that," Paula whispered back. "The stable yard is to the left of us." Paula turned on a flashlight. Unsteadily, Izzy crunched forward across the gravel.

I shouldn't be doing this, every inch of her body screamed out, and yet she was powerless to stop herself. Like a robot she followed Paula, walking across the grass, ducking under tree branches... until finally they turned a corner and the unmistakeable smell of horses hung in the air.

"Here we are," Paula whispered. "Here's a plan. I suggest we look in the office together, then I'll leave you and go on to look around the rest of the yard. I know my way around here and you don't. We can meet back in the car in ten minutes. Okay?"

Izzy nodded. She looked at the red-brick building of the office and took a deep breath. "Okay, let's go."

Stealthily, they crossed the yard. Izzy desperately tried to stifle the sound of her feet on the gravel as Paula swung open the door to the office. Izzy walked inside and automatically reached up to find a switch to turn the light on.

"Don't do that!" Paula hissed. "Someone'll be out here in a flash if we turn on the lights."

"Sorry." Izzy blushed in the darkness, instantly feeling foolish. "It's just that it's so dark in here."

"Which is why we use the flashlight." Paula flipped it on and let the rays of light bounce around the room. "Filing cabinet, desk... where shall we start?" Paula walked over to the desk and pulled open the top drawer. Holding the flashlight in one hand, she rummaged through the drawer with the other.

Izzy looked around her in a panic – she didn't know what to do.

"Quick," Paula hissed. "You take the filing cabinet."

"Er, but what are we looking for?" Izzy asked uncertainly.

"I don't know – anything." Paula threw her hands in the air.

Edgily, Izzy made her way over to the other side of the room and began systematically pulling out drawer after drawer. Papers upon papers loomed out at her... veterinary receipts, training bills, breeding certificates. She pushed the drawers back into place.

"Nothing useful in there," Paula grimaced, pushing in the last drawer of the desk. "I'll leave you with the flashlight."

"Sure." Izzy heard the faint click of the door shutting behind Paula. She swallowed hard, then took a deep breath as she stooped down, fiddling with the bottom drawer. Her fingers were all thumbs. She tried to pull it open, but it was locked. Desperately, Izzy looked around her, hoping she might see a set of keys hanging on a hook. She flashed the flashlight around the room and made her way over to the desk.

Eventually, her legs gave way and she sat down in

the chair. Vacantly, she stared in front of her – a jar of pens, paperclips, in-tray... the beam flashed around the desk top, landing neatly on each of the objects and then moving on. And then her heart missed a beat as her gaze came to rest on a single slip of paper with writing on it. As Izzy leaned forward to get a closer look, the words swam in front of her eyes. It was only two lines, but what she saw completely took her breath away. She hadn't really had a chance to think about what they might find at Joe Hagan's farm, but what she had found looked like evidence that they hadn't had a wasted trip...

Izzy took a deep breath. It seemed as though she had found the missing connection – the only way this man could be getting to the horses at Graytops without actually being there himself. Now all they had to do was prove it.

Izzy shivered as she stared at the desk. Then, slowly, she reached forward and picked up the piece of paper. Switching off her flashlight, she just sat there for a moment, soaking up the darkness. Then she heard a sound outside – the loud crunching of footsteps on gravel. Quickly she ducked down under the desk as the room was flooded with light.

"I thought I heard a noise coming from in here," a man's voice boomed out.

Izzy felt sick. It had to be Joe Hagan. And if he came in any further, he'd be sure to find her.

"You must have been imagining it, Joe," came a woman's voice.

"Hmm, maybe," the man said, "but you can never be too careful."

Izzy peeped out from under the desk and drew her

breath in sharply. She hadn't closed the top drawer of the filing cabinet and it stood there, wide open, for all to see. If they noticed that, they'd be sure to come into the room. She held her breath, hoping against hope... One... two... three...

"There's nothing in here, Meg. I must be going crazy in my old age," the man's voice came again. "Let's get back to the house."

The light went off and, once again, the office was shrouded in darkness. Izzy didn't move. It was hot outside, but her teeth were chattering. She had to get back to the car before anything else happened. Her legs felt like jelly. She'd almost been caught – and by Joe Hagan – the man masterminding this whole abomination. And what about Paula? Was she all right? Izzy didn't like to think what Joe Hagan might do to her if she was caught.

Izzy pulled up the sleeve of her shirt. The numbers on her watch dial glowed, plain and clear – 10 o'clock. She should have been back at the car by now.

Izzy uncurled herself from her crouched position and stretched out her legs. She got to her feet and peered out of the office window. The yard was as dark as pitch. It was now or never. Slowly, very slowly, Izzy turned the door handle and made her bid for escape...

12

DISAGREEMENTS

Kate looked at her watch and then back at the wall again. It was ten o'clock and Paula and Izzy still weren't back. Where were they? One thing was for sure – they were going to be late getting back to Graytops and Sally was going to be furious.

"Come on, come on," she muttered, willing the two faces to appear at the top of the wall.

And then she heard something – the breathless sound of someone running and a scraping sound as someone launched themselves at the wall... and then there was a face – Paula's. Kate sat there, waiting for Izzy to appear, but there was no sign of her. Swiftly, she unbuckled her seat belt and called out.

"What's happened? Where's Izzy?"

"Ssshh," Paula said. "They'll hear you."

"They? Who?" Kate said, starting to panic.

"Joe Hagan and his wife... they're out there."

"You mean, they're in the yard and you've just left Izzy inside?" Kate was shocked. "Then I'm going to have to go in and get her."

"No way," Paula said. "Look, give it ten more minutes, then if she's not out, we'll go in after her."

*

It was the longest ten minutes of Kate's life. Every thirty seconds she kept looking at her watch until eventually she said that enough was enough. But then Paula grabbed her back.

"Listen... I can hear something," she said triumphantly.

And then Kate heard it too – a scrabbling sound from the other side of the wall, and then Izzy's face appeared, whiter than white.

"Oh Izzy," Kate cried. "You didn't get caught... thank goodness you're safe."

"It was a close call," Izzy said, her confidence returning now that she was outside the walls. Breathlessly, she jumped down, brushing her hands as she walked over to the car.

"I've been worried sick," Kate said. "What is it, Izzy? You're looking very strange. Did you find something?"

"Well, look, I don't know how to put this," Izzy said, turning to Paula and Kate. "But yes, I did. I think it could be important." She dug deep into her pocket. "It's not the drugs or anything like that."

Kate looked puzzled as Izzy handed her the piece of paper.

"I found it on the desk inside," Izzy said.

Kate uncrumpled it and took in the writing.

"But this – it's... it's Ted's name, and a mobile number," Kate gasped.

"Ted must be the missing link," Izzy said simply. "Why else would he have given Joe Hagan his mobile number when he could have just been phoned at Graytops?"

"It would explain everything," Paula gasped.

Izzy nodded. "It does seem a coincidence that Ted was the only person kept on at the stables after the first doping, and then it happened again... I just don't know why we didn't think of him before."

"Probably because Sally placed so much faith in him," Kate said gloomily.

"I've never liked him," Izzy said emphatically. "Remember how he was with me over that saddle?"

"Yes, but that doesn't make him guilty, does it?" Kate said.

"No, but this does," Izzy said slowly. "Who'd have thought it? All we have to do now is catch him."

"Whoa, now hold on a minute," Paula had been quiet during this exchange but now she stepped in. "What do you mean, *catch him*? You know the best thing to do is go to Sally with this piece of paper."

"It's not enough," Kate said simply. "Sally would never take it at face value – she'd give him the benefit of the doubt and speak to him first and that would give him a chance to wiggle out of it. What do you think, Izzy? You know the Bryant family as well as I do – they think the world of Ted, don't they?"

"Yes, they do." Izzy nodded. "And I have to say I agree with everything you've said. Besides, what would we say? We couldn't tell Sally where we'd been tonight – she'd flip her lid."

"But what about Seattle?" Paula looked worried. "You'd be leaving her totally at Ted's mercy."

"Not if we protect her," Kate stepped in. "Not if we watch Ted night and day."

Paula's eyes narrowed. "It sounds like you're scared to me – scared of putting your neck on the line for Seattle."

"We're not scared." Izzy's eyes flashed. "We're just being sensible."

And that was all that was said on the matter. Without saying another word, Paula started up the car and drove Izzy and Kate off into the night.

*

By the time Paula dropped Izzy and Kate off at Graytops that evening it was already twenty past ten and no one was saying very much. It wasn't that they had fallen out exactly, it was just that they had such different ideas about what they should do. And while Izzy and Kate could see where Paula was coming from, they were adamant that they couldn't, just couldn't tell Sally – at least not yet.

As Izzy and Kate walked up the driveway, they realized they were going to have to think of a very good excuse for being late.

"Maybe Sally'll be in bed," Izzy muttered hopefully.

"I think that's highly unlikely." Kate raised her eyebrows.

"Hmm, I guess you're right," Izzy said as they turned the corner of the driveway. "Uh-oh, the lights are on, I guess we'd better face the music."

Izzy and Kate jogged the last hundred yards of the driveway and, running up the steps to the house, pushed open the front door and walked down the hallway.

"Izzy... Kate..." The sight of three worried-looking faces greeted them. "Where on earth have you been? We've been worried," Sally cried. "We thought you might have had an accident."

"Oh no, we're very sorry," Izzy said, looking across at Kate.

"Sorry?" Sally looked unsatisfied. "But the movie finished ages ago."

"Um, er, we lost track of the time," Izzy said feebly. "We went for a burger with Paula."

"But I told you you had to be back by ten," Sally said firmly. "Just wait until I see Paula, I'm going to give her a piece of my mind."

"No, don't do that," Izzy said hurriedly, and then, seeing the angry look on Sally's face, she changed her tone of voice. "I mean, we're sorry and..."

"Just head up to bed," Sally sighed tiredly. "We'll talk about this in the morning."

13

TROUBLE

"All right, all right," Sally held her hands in the air. "I've heard enough explaining for one day." It was early on Thursday morning, and Sally looked tired as she ran a hand through her hair. "Okay, so you lost track of the time, but you did have us very worried." Izzy and Kate sat at the kitchen table, looking shamefaced.

"I don't have any more time to discuss it," Sally said wearily. "I've got more important things to think about – like Seattle's race on Tuesday. So, let's put it behind us and go join Courtney and Megan at the barn," she said, getting up as the ring of the telephone sounded across the room.

Kate and Izzy looked relieved as they watched her reach for the receiver.

"Hello Doug, yes darling, everything's fine..." Sally waved Kate and Izzy away and gratefully, they bolted for the back door. Quickly, they turned into the woods and headed toward the barn.

"Courtney... Megan," Izzy cried.

"Oh, it's you," Courtney huffed.

"Don't be like that, Courtney," Izzy said.

"Yes, well, you put Mom in a really bad mood and she's taking it out on us-"

Thud! Splash!

Courtney's attention was quickly deflected away from the conversation as Garnet gave one kick of his foreleg and his water bucket went flying. Water seeped across the ground.

"Oh man!" Courtney cried, rushing over as the horse went on to put his foot in the bucket. "You stupid old nag," she cried affectionately, slowly lifting his hoof out before he could get into a panic. Then she turned back to Izzy and Kate. "Can you go and start mucking out?" she said. "Ted's already out on the oval. We'll meet him there."

Izzy was happy that Courtney's bad mood had passed so quickly, but as for seeing Ted – it made Izzy shiver to even hear his name. They hadn't caught sight of the stable manager since their discovery last night – and Izzy wasn't entirely sure that she wanted to...

*

Izzy and Kate kept as close a watch on Ted as possible over the next few days and in fact, he surprised them – surprised them by the fact that he didn't so much as go anywhere near Seattle Surprise. He pretty much left Sally to look after her. On Saturday morning, there was a surprise waiting for Izzy and Kate in the shape of the ride they'd been dreaming of. Sally said they could join the exercise string – riding Sugarfoot and Lark's Song. Izzy and Kate were very excited and were doing an extra good job of grooming the two racehorses.

"I'm going to go and get Lark Song's saddle," Izzy said.

"Okay, I'll see you in a minute then," Kate responded, continuing to brush the beautiful coat of the horse in front of her.

As Izzy came out of the barn, the brightness of the day hit her, and she held up her hand to shield her eyes from the sun.

Quickly, she made her way across the stable yard, humming gently to herself as she went to enter the tack room. Then she stopped still for a moment. She thought she could hear a voice, but Kate was back at the barn and everyone else had already left for the training oval. She listened again but there was nothing. She must have just been imagining it and, thinking no more of it, she disappeared into the tack room. Her eyes ran over the different name plates, looking for the right saddle – Seattle Surprise, Sugarfoot, Tobago Bay... she read the names aloud. There it was – Lark's Song. Izzy reached up and took down the saddle. Then, she hurried back outside. She was just about to walk into the barn when she heard a voice again... and suddenly, she realized that she hadn't been imagining it. There was definitely a voice – and it was coming from the office. It sounded like someone was on the telephone. The door was closed, but the window was open and whoever was talking was doing so in low tones.

Izzy stopped still. Just who could be in there? She crept across the yard until she was just a little way away from the door of the office. Could she chance it and get any closer? Izzy moved forward until she was just inches away from the glass. And then she took a deep breath. On the count of three... one, two, three. She twisted her neck and looked into the office...

Ted! He had his back turned to her and his voice was muffled. She tried to hear what he was saying. He sounded angry. Suddenly he turned to face the window, and Izzy ducked. Now that he had turned around, she could hear everything.

"I'll fight you every step of the way...

I can't get you that kind of money...

But that would kill her."

Izzy's heart began to beat faster and suddenly everything started swimming in front of her. Ted was talking about killing Seattle! Izzy's legs felt like jelly and her stomach was churning as she crouched there, leaning against the wall for support. She had to get away before he caught her listening. One foot in front of the other – that was all it took. One step, two steps... and then there was a call that chilled her bones.

"Who's that... who's there?"

Izzy froze to the spot. Before she even had a chance to make her move, the office door was flung open and Ted stood there, looking at her.

"What do you think you're doing?" he said, an angry look flashing over his face.

"Um, I came to get Lark's Song's saddle and tripped..." Izzy stumbled around for the words, not knowing what else to say.

A dawning realization crossed Ted's face. "You've been eavesdropping, haven't you? Listening in to my phone call?" And suddenly he looked very angry... menacing even.

"No, I wasn't, I mean... I was just coming to look for you – Kate's been having problems tacking up Sugarfoot – I didn't hear anything, I mean..." Izzy felt herself getting hysterical.

"All right, all right, calm down," Ted said. "It's not the end of the world." And then he broke into a crooked smile and the falseness of it all almost made Izzy choke. "I'll come and give you a hand. Here, let me carry that." He went to take the saddle out of Izzy's arms but Izzy shrank back.

"What's up? I'm not going to hurt you." He looked puzzled. "Come on, let's go and get Sugarfoot tacked up."

"No, I mean, that's fine," Izzy stammered. "We'll be all right, I mean..."

"Look, either you want my help or you don't," Ted said firmly, leading the way.

It was too late to stop him and all that Izzy could do was turn and follow after him.

"Cat got your tongue?" Ted said as they walked into the barn.

"No, I... I..."

"Well anyway, here we are," Ted said. "So what

97

seems to be the problem?"

"Problem?" Kate stood up straight at Sugarfoot's shoulder. "What problem?"

"I told Ted how you were having problems tacking up Sugarfoot." Izzy widened her eyes, willing her friend to go along with it.

"I'm not having any problems," Kate frowned. "Sugarfoot's fine. What are you going on about, Izzy?" And then, seeing Izzy's pale face, she blustered on. "I mean... I was having problems... well, for a few minutes anyway, but I'm all right now... Sugarfoot's calmed down and-"

"So you don't need any help after all?" Ted interrupted. "I don't know – you two girls."

He shrugged his shoulders and just stood there.

"I must have made a mistake, yes that's it – a mistake," Izzy laughed falsely, the relief flooding through her as she realized that Ted had momentarily forgotten about her overhearing his phone call.

"Well, if you don't need me, I'll see you both out on the oval then," Ted shrugged.

"Yes, all right, on the oval," Izzy said.

Ted looked at her curiously and then turned quickly and walked off down the aisle. As he disappeared, Izzy leaned back against the partition wall.

"What is it? What's going on, Izzy? What's this stuff about me having problems tacking up?"

"You're not going to believe this, Kate..."

And suddenly Izzy let everything flood out – everything that she'd heard Ted say – until finally she finished with the part about killing Seattle Surprise.

"Kill her!" Kate gasped. "But... but he can't do that..."

98

"But he's going to," Izzy said, trying to gather her cool.

"Look, are you sure you heard all this right, Izzy?" Kate questioned her. "What exactly did he say?"

"Just what I told you," Izzy said angrily. "If you don't believe me..."

"Of course I believe you," Kate said firmly. "But just what are we going to do?"

14

DRASTIC MEASURES

That evening, Courtney walked into the den where the other three girls were sitting in front of the TV. Izzy and Kate hadn't said a word since they'd got in. They'd still been dwelling on the events of the afternoon and wondering what to do.

"Phone call for you, Izzy," Courtney said.

"For me?" Izzy looked startled.

"Yes, I think it's Paula," she frowned. "Don't let Mom know she's calling here – she's still pretty mad about the other night."

"Oh right... thanks." Quickly, Izzy hurried out into the kitchen and picked up the receiver. She took a deep breath. "Hello?"

"Izzy? It's me, Paula..."

"Thank goodness you called," Izzy breathed.

"Why? What's happened?" Paula's voice came quickly.

"I can't explain now," Izzy said. "But it's Ted – it's definitely Ted who's doping the horses. I heard him on the phone. He's said he's going to kill Seattle. What on earth do we do?"

Paula was quiet.

"Are you still there, Paula?" Izzy whispered.

"Yes, yes, I'm here," she breathed. "All you can do is tell Sally. Tell her everything."

"Yes, I suppose we should," Izzy said, trying to summon up courage. "Yes, of course you're right."

"Do you want me to come over and see you at the farm?" Paula said.

"No, I don't think that's a good idea," Izzy said quickly, thinking about what Courtney had said about Sally still being mad at Paula. She didn't want to make everything so much worse. "Paula... Paula, are you there?"

"Yes, I'm here," Paula said.

"You do understand, don't you?"

"Yeah, yeah, I suppose so," Paula said.

"Look, I'd better go," Izzy said. "But don't worry, I'll make sure that Sally's told."

As Izzy put down the phone, she stopped for a moment. Paula had sounded really hurt and Izzy felt bad. Paula had been the first real friend they'd made out here. Still, there wasn't anything she could do about that now. Chewing on her bottom lip, Izzy made her way back into the den to join the others.

*

101

"Now? You think I should tell her now?" Izzy called across the jumping paddock from where she was sitting on the back of Prince.

"Well, you chickened out of it last night, and now seems as good a time as any," Kate answered breathlessly, cantering Garnet in a neat circle around the jumping paddock.

"One more time around and then I'm done." Izzy gritted her teeth as she turned Prince for the course laid out in front of her. Kicking him hard, she turned him for the brush hurdle. They went flying over the first jump and Izzy switched her attention to the parallel bars. Gracefully she soared around the course, jumping over fence after fence in easy succession.

"Wow, Izzy, that was really fast," Kate laughed.

"Call it tension," Izzy said, jumping to the ground and leading Prince off by the reins. "Wish me luck."

"Fingers crossed..." Kate called across, biting on her bottom lip. They'd decided it would be better if just one person told Sally what they knew – one person would be able to explain everything so much more clearly than two. Kate had won the toss of the coin, and had elected to stay in the background. Now she felt bad – she didn't envy Izzy this task. They should really be doing this together.

"Look, I'm going to come with you, Izzy," she called.

"What?" Izzy answered.

'I'm going to come with you," Kate repeated herself.

"Great," Izzy grinned. "I thought you'd never offer. Come on then."

The two girls turned from the paddock and led the

ponies back into the yard.

"Hi there," Sally waved, from where she was hosing down Tobago Bay. "How did you do out there?"

"Oh, really good, thanks," Izzy said, feeling the butterflies in the pit of her stomach. She tied Garnet to a ring in the wall. Kate did the same with Prince. Izzy gritted her teeth. It was now or never.

"Sally, do you think we could talk to you?" Izzy walked over, her hands thrust deep into her pockets.

"Um, look, can it wait until a little later, Izzy?" Sally said. "I'm in kind of a rush right now – especially with Ted away for a few days."

"Ted's not going to be around?" Izzy glanced at Kate, looking shocked. This changed everything. How could he dope Seattle if he wasn't even going to be around?

"Why the surprise?" Sally raised her eyebrows quizzically.

"Um, well, no real reason, but why isn't he going to be around? It seems a strange time to go away – with Seattle's race just around the corner."

"Yeah, well that's his business," Sally said firmly.

Izzy didn't know what to say; thoughts ran through her mind.

"Have you left Garnet and Prince over there?" Sally wrinkled up her brow.

"Um, well, yes," Izzy nodded. "We were going to rub them down in a minute."

"Yeah, well don't leave them out too long. Now, I better finish up here, Izzy," Sally said as she turned back to Tobago Bay.

Izzy looked at Kate. It seemed pointless just to

stand there and so they walked across the yard, back to the ponies.

"I didn't feel I could say anything after all that." Izzy shot Kate a gloomy look.

"No, I mean we could hardly tell her that we think Ted's going to dope Seattle when he's not even going to be around." Kate looked gloomy as she leaned forward to undo Garnet's girth. "So, where do you think Ted's going? What do you think he's up to?"

"I dunno," Izzy said. "But there's one thing I can be sure of – we haven't heard the end of this. Just because Ted's not going to be around it doesn't mean Seattle's any safer."

"You don't think so?" Kate said.

"No, I don't. It just gives him the perfect alibi. Ted won't go far. In fact, I wouldn't be at all surprised if he didn't try to sneak back into the stable yard when there's no one around."

"Yes, but there's always someone around," Kate said thoughtfully.

"Not at night there isn't," Izzy raised her eyebrows. "Why can't Sally smell a rat?" she cried out in frustration. "Look, there's only one thing we can do – we're going to have to guard Seattle all day, and the night before her race too. The security guard can't be everywhere at once."

"What? But Sally would never go for that," Kate said.

"No, I don't think she would," Izzy said. "So we're not going to tell her." Izzy raised her eyebrows. "We'll stay in Seattle's stall without her knowing. That's the only way we can be sure that Seattle will be safe."

"Well maybe, but don't you think we should get

Megan and Courtney involved?" Kate said uncertainly.

"No, definitely not – we know how they feel about Ted," Izzy said.

Kate opened her mouth to say something, and closed it again. Izzy was right. If they told Courtney and Megan it would mean explaining everything – all they'd found out about Ted, where they'd been that night – and that might ruin everything. Besides, the fewer people that got involved right now, the better.

"Yes Izzy." Kate took a deep breath. "Yes, I guess you're right."

15

NIGHT-WATCH

"Ssshh," Izzy called across to Kate. "If we get caught, we'll be in big trouble."

The days had passed quickly – guarding Seattle had taken up most of their time. But nothing had happened to her, and now the night before Seattle's race lay ahead of them. Quietly Izzy and Kate tiptoed down the stairs, making their way to the front door, stopping only to put their sneakers on.

"Come on," Izzy murmured.

It was 10 o'clock and the moon was high in the sky as they made their way through the trees that evening. They waited until the security guard had passed the arched entrance to the barn, and then they walked forward. Quickly, they avoided the sensory floodlights and walked across to the barn where Seattle was stabled, drawing back the door and closing it behind them before tiptoeing down the aisle. The little gray mare seemed surprised to see them when they looked in over her stall door. She was lying in the straw, but was not yet asleep. She gave a little nicker and got to her feet.

"Ssshh, hush now, settle down, Seattle." Izzy turned to Kate. "Perhaps this isn't such a good idea after all – we don't want to unsettle her the night before her big race."

"She'll be all right," Kate said. "She'll settle back down and go to sleep in a minute, and then we can slip in there and bed down for the night."

"Yes, you're right," Izzy said thoughtfully. "And surely if anything was going to happen to Seattle, it would have happened by now."

"Well, you just don't know, do you?" Kate said.

Izzy nodded and looked back over Seattle's stall door.

No one would believe that the gentle, gray creature lying asleep in the straw was such a powerful racehorse.

"Come on," Izzy yawned.

Kate nodded. Seattle's stall was lit by the little window at the back, and the moonlight flooded in across the floor as they stepped inside.

"Perfect." Izzy fluffed up the straw. "Who could ask for a more comfortable watch post?"

"We're going to be exhausted by the morning though." Kate gave a wry smile. "Still, I guess it'll be worth it."

"Ssshh..." Izzy put her finger to her lip. "Did you hear something?"

"No." Kate looked nervous. She sat upright and listened but all she could hear were the usual horse sounds of a stables.

"It was probably nothing," Izzy said, settling back down.

The two girls sat in the dark, whispering to each other. They had made allowances for the fact that they would get bored, but they hadn't made allowances for the tiredness that would creep in.

"Kate... Kate, are you awake?" After five minutes of silence, Izzy nudged her friend. There was no movement and, as Izzy leaned over her friend's body, she could hear gentle little snores.

She shrugged her shoulders. Typical. So much for them both keeping an all-night vigil. Now there was even more responsibility on her shoulders.

"Oh Kate..." she murmured under her breath. The peaceful quiet of the stable lulled Izzy and, as she sat there, she shifted her weight around to relieve the boredom.

Izzy felt her eyelids closing, getting heavier and heavier. She couldn't help herself – she was drifting off to sleep. And then she thought she heard a noise. Had she imagined it – or dreamed it? She sat bolt upright. There it was again, only this time she knew for certain that she wasn't imagining or dreaming. Izzy felt her heart racing faster. Somebody was pulling back the iron door of the barn. A grating sound echoed down the aisle.

Izzy froze to the spot. This was what they were there for – to stop Ted from getting near Seattle, but now that it was actually happening, she didn't know what to do.

"Kate... Kate," she whispered as she shook her friend's shoulder. "Can you hear that?"

"Uh..." Kate sat upright and rubbed her tired eyes. "I must have fallen asleep."

"Never mind that," Izzy whispered. "Can you hear a noise?"

Kate listened carefully, but there was only silence. "No, it's nothing, Izzy," she murmured. "You must be imagining it. You know, I think we should go back to the house."

"Ssshh." Izzy clutched at Kate's arm as the grating sound echoed around the barn. And this time, Izzy and Kate froze, eyes wide open.

"Oh my goodness, Izzy. What do we do now?" Kate whispered, starting to panic.

"I don't know." Izzy mouthed the words, her calm rapidly evaporating with every passing second. The noise was getting louder and louder.

"I'm going to confront him," Izzy said firmly. And before she could think twice about it, she jumped to her feet.

"Ted?" she cried out. "Ted, is that you?"

*

It was silent for a moment, but not silent enough. Izzy could definitely hear something and as she looked ahead of her, she could make out a shadowy figure in front of her.

"Ted?" she called again.

109

Whoever it was was dressed in black, but it was so dark that Izzy couldn't really see more than that. In a split second, the figure had sprung into action and was gone – fleeing out of the barn in a flash.

Izzy didn't stop to think. She pulled herself to her senses and followed suit – down the aisle and out of the door in a flash. The sensory lights flooded the yard as she sprinted across the gravel... to the other side, past the tack room and over the gate, into the paddocks beyond.

Izzy caught a glimpse of him, heading into the black night. He was getting away. Her lungs felt as though they would burst, she was panting so hard. She could hear voices behind her, but still she kept on running...

Then she drew to a halt, gasping to catch her breath as she realized what a hopeless task it was. Izzy stared in front of her and then back at the stable yard. The lights looked comforting and it didn't take long for Izzy to decide to go back. Wearily she walked across the paddocks. As she climbed over the gate, Kate and the security guard rushed toward her.

"Izzy... thank goodness you're all right." The relief was written all over Kate's face. "You shouldn't have run off like that." She hugged her friend.

"Yes, well, as you can see, I'm fine." Izzy shrugged her friend's arm off, feeling embarrassed. Then, seeing Kate's hurt look, she gave her a little smile. "He was a little too fast for me, that's all."

"Yes, well it's lucky that he was," Kate said.

"It looks like he's long gone," the security guard joined in, looking worried.

Izzy looked over Kate's shoulder in the direction

of the house. She could see some lights in the distance. That meant that Sally and Courtney and Megan would be across in no time at all.

"Did you get a look at him?" the security guard asked.

I don't know, I mean..." Izzy had half of her concentration focused on the conversation and the other half focused on the track that led from the house. She turned back to the security guard. "Well, no, not really. I couldn't see very much of him."

Izzy looked back again and this time she saw Sally coming through the archway, closely followed by Courtney and Megan.

"What is it? What's going on?" Sally drew to a halt by the group, her eyes wide and her hair tousled from sleep.

"Someone was trying to get into Seattle's stable," the security guard started. "Though just how anyone got into the grounds, I don't know. These girls caught him going into the barn."

"But... but Seattle – is she all right? Izzy, Kate, tell me what happened." Sally looked alarmed.

"Seattle's fine," Izzy said quickly. "He wasn't able to get anywhere near her – not with us there."

"Oh thank goodness... thank goodness she's safe. But what were you doing out here? Are you girls all right?" Sally looked at Izzy and Kate. "You shouldn't have been out here at night."

"I know, um... but... well, we were sleeping in Seattle's stable. You see, we were worried about her," Izzy broke in.

"Worried?" Sally hugged Izzy and Kate close to her. "Oh, you silly girls. Thank goodness nothing happened to either of you. You could have put yourselves in real danger. Enough's enough." Sally covered her face in her hands. "We can't go on like this..." Her voice broke into hysterics. "I should have known that everything was going too smoothly with Seattle's training. I shouldn't have let Ted go – we really needed him here..."

Kate and Izzy looked at each other. They didn't know what to say.

"You couldn't have stopped him from going," Courtney said, looking at Megan for support.

"No, I know," Sally said, more calmly now that she had composed herself. "Look, let's go check on Seattle. I want to make sure she really is all right."

The girls followed Sally into the barn and down the aisle. Izzy and Kate felt relieved as they looked in over Seattle's stable. Unaware of the commotion that had been going on around her, the little gray mare was sleeping soundly.

"Thank goodness for that," Sally breathed. "She's fine. She turned to the security guard. "Why weren't you guarding the barn?"

"I thought you wanted me to patrol the grounds," he said gruffly.

"Yes, well, I suppose I did," Sally said. "But from now until morning I want you to stand outside this barn. I'll need to inform the police but I can call them in the morning. Now come on girls, let's get across to the house. We all need to get some rest..."

16

CLEVEDON PARK

No one was in very high spirits as they sat down to breakfast the next morning. In fact, no one so much as said a word. Courtney just sat there, stirring her cereal. Megan stared vacantly out of the window, and Sally seemed to be in another world completely. As she got up and left the room, Courtney turned to Izzy.

"You know, we're really mad at you. Why didn't you include us in your plans? We could have kept watch with you. We trusted you with everything about Graytops... why couldn't you trust us?"

"Well..." Izzy didn't know what to say. How could she tell them that they'd thought about it, and then decided not to because of Ted? She felt relieved when Sally came back into the room and she could change the subject. "Did Seattle get off to the track all right?"

"Fine." Sally nodded. "The trailer came to get her at five."

"She will be safe, won't she?" Courtney said, her face as white as a sheet.

"Of course she will," Sally said. "Hank Brewer's been driving for us for years. He won't let her out of his sight. I would have liked to have gone in the trailer with her, but with Ted gone there's no one else to see to the other horses here. Anyway, we'll get to the track by noon," Sally said wearily. "And I'm sure that Seattle will be safe."

But Izzy could tell from the way that Sally was gripping the handle of her coffee cup that there was no definite guarantee of that.

Sally buried her head in her hands and looked up again. "Look Izzy, I know that you must have gone over this again and again, but the police may want to question you later. Did you catch a glimpse of this man at all? Is there anything you can remember about him?"

"Well," Izzy faltered. "It was so dark, I couldn't really see. He wasn't very tall." Hopelessly she stared down at her feet.

Sally sighed. "Well, if anything should come to you – anything at all – you must tell us. I know that it's scary, but anything you remember could hold the key to it all."

"I know, and of course I will," Izzy said firmly. If only she could say she had definitely seen Ted.

"Don't worry." Sally patted Izzy on the shoulder. "Let's get over to the stable yard now and start mucking out."

"Well actually, Sally," Izzy hesitated. This was her moment.

"Yes," Sally turned back.

It was now or never. Izzy took a deep breath. "It's

just something that Kate and I have been thinking..."

"Go on."

"Well," Izzy stammered. "We were wondering – I mean – where's Ted at the moment?"

"Ted?" Sally looked surprised. "What's that got to do with anything? You're not thinking Ted have been our night-time intruder, are you?" She let out a low laugh.

"Well..." Izzy hesitated.

Sally looked suspiciously at her. "You are joking, aren't you?"

"You've got to admit that it's a little strange that he's gone away for a few days." Kate stepped in. "I mean – this is Seattle's big race, isn't it?" She started to turn red as she tried to figure out an easy way of saying things. But there was no nice way of putting it. "And he knows the farm from back to front – it would be easy for him to slip past the security guard, and he's been around all of the other times and..." Kate was about to go on, but Sally interrupted her.

"It's not Ted." Sally took a deep breath.

"But how can you be so sure?" Kate said.

"I just know, that's all," Sally said, patting Kate on the shoulder. "Now, come on. We've got work to do."

And with that, she left the room, followed by Courtney and Megan. Kate turned to Izzy.

"Well, that's it, we've blown it. No one's ever going to believe us about Ted now – we've just managed to let him off the hook. He's gotten away with all this completely scot-free..."

*

It was just noon when Sally finally turned into the parking lot at Clevedon Park Racetrack. It was already busy and there were rows and rows of cars ahead of them. Izzy and Kate followed Sally's lead through the turnstiles and into the grounds. They were feeling upset, and Courtney and Megan were acting distant.

Sally handed everyone their badges as they came to a halt in front of a bronze horse.

"Okay, well Seattle's not running until the third race." Sally turned to the group. "So I'm going to go and check up on her. Why don't you all go and soak up the atmosphere? We'll meet over there before Seattle's race." She pointed to the right of the grandstand in front of them.

"Okay." Courtney and Megan nodded.

As Sally hurried away, the girls stood awkwardly together.

"I guess that's the winning post then?" Izzy said finally, pointing to the red and white pole directly in front of the manicured lawns.

Courtney nodded. "Yeah, anyway, now that you have your bearings, we can go take a look at the horses."

Izzy and Kate nodded, following Courtney and Megan through a white-railed gate to where a man was checking entry tickets. Izzy flashed him her junior badge and slipped through, and then they walked past the parade ring and in the direction of the stables. Finally they got as far as they could go. They stood, watching from behind the railings.

It was already really busy. Grooms were leading sheeted horses around; people were running this way and that, and camera crews were wheeling equipment around, preparing for the live coverage of the day's racing. And then there were the horses – chestnuts, bays, grays – every possible color.

"Let's go and find Seattle." Courtney and Megan ducked under the railings. "Look, Izzy... Kate... why don't we split up for an hour? It might be hard for the four of us to stay together with all these crowds. We could meet on the right of the grandstand in half an hour."

"Yes, good idea," Izzy breathed a sigh of relief. It would be nice to have some space away from the twins and, as they walked away, she immediately started to feel better.

"Well, we've totally blown it with Courtney and Megan, you know," Kate said finally

"I guess," Izzy answered. "Hey," she yelped as someone trod on her foot.

"Sorry," the man apologized.

"That's OK." As Izzy smiled up at him, she spotted something, or rather someone, across the lawn and in the distance. "Hey, look over there. Isn't that Paula?"

"Where?" Kate squinted into the sun as she looked over to where Izzy was pointing. Paula was hurrying away, threading her way through the crowd. They hadn't spoken to their friend since that phone conversation when Izzy had promised to tell Sally – they owed it to her to tell her about everything that had happened since then.

"Come on," Kate said. "Let's go and see her."

"Paula... Paula..." Kate called breathlessly, darting this way and that through the crowds.

It looked at first as though they'd never catch her.

There were just too many people and the noise was too great, but then something must have caught Paula's attention because she looked back over her shoulder.

"Paula... Paula!" Kate and Izzy stopped right in front of her.

"Oh, it's you guys. What are you two doing here?" she frowned.

"It's Seattle's big race – remember?" Izzy said.

"Oh yes, so it is." Paula stopped short.

Izzy and Kate looked at each other, puzzled by Paula's reaction. Surely she must have remembered that Seattle was racing today. It was all they'd talked about for the last couple of weeks.

"Let's hope she runs well then," Paula smiled, but her manner was still aloof. "Look, I'm really busy. What was it you wanted anyway?"

"Well, nothing really – just to say hello," Izzy shrugged, puzzled by Paula's unfriendly attitude. "And to tell you what's been going on at Graytops as well."

"There was an intruder at the farm last night," Kate said breathlessly. "We started to tell Sally that we thought it could be Ted, but then she went nuts... said it couldn't possibly be him."

"Well, did you tell her you'd seen his face?" Paula said.

"Well no, because we didn't," Izzy said.

"Well, you shouldn't be surprised then that she didn't believe you," Paula said firmly. "You should have told her about Ted when I told you to – right back when we found that piece of paper."

"Yes, well you're probably right," Izzy said, looking closely at Paula and noticing that a sweat had broken out on her forehead. "Paula? Paula, are you all right?"

"Yes, of course I'm fine." Paula smiled weakly.

"Seattle has no idea of the fuss that's been going on around her," Kate joined in. "She got here safely so at least she should be all right today – after all, Ted's not around."

"All right?" Paula sneered. "Well, if she is all right it won't be because of you."

Izzy and Kate looked shocked, but before they could say anything more, Paula had started again.

"Ted may not be here, but that doesn't change the fact that Joe Hagan's at Clevedon Park, does it? It'll be your fault if Seattle's found with benzocaine in her system like the last horse..."

"Uh, look, let's all calm down," Kate said, not wanting to fight openly.

"Yes, you're right," Paula said angrily. "We should calm down. In fact, I'm not standing around arguing with you pair of fools. I've got a job to do."

And with that, she was gone – disappearing into the crowd.

"What was all that about?" Kate looked confused. "It was like she was a different person."

"I don't know," Izzy said, feeling hurt. "Do you think she's not feeling well, or something? Did you see the way she was sweating?"

"Yes, her bangs were soaking," Kate said doubtfully. "But to speak to us like that. I thought she was our friend."

Izzy snorted. "We might be younger than her but she didn't need to talk to us like we were idiots and just what did she mean that it would be our fault if Seattle was found with benzocaine-" Izzy stopped

119

short. She and Kate looked at each other. "Benzocaine!"

"But no one's supposed to know about that drug," Kate stammered. "No one except for the family. Oh Izzy..."

Izzy paled as she looked at Kate. "We've been barking up completely the wrong tree. We've got to get to Seattle – and quick..."

17

A DISMAL DISCOVERY

It seemed to take Izzy and Kate an eternity to get from the lawn in front of the grandstand to the stables. Impatiently, they pushed their way through the crowds... through the gate... past the parade ring... until, out of breath, they dashed down the track to the stables.

"Hey you kids – you can't go down there," the security guard called after them, but there was no stopping Izzy and Kate. On and on they ran until they were at the stables. There were some surprised faces, and some irritated ones too as Izzy and Kate swerved through the oncoming horses.

"There's Sally," Izzy panted.

"Sally... Sally," Kate cried.

"What in the world..."

"There isn't time," Izzy cried. "Where's Seattle?"

"She's in that box there," Sally said. "Paula's with

her – what is this?"

Izzy and Kate didn't stop to answer her. As they reached Seattle's box they drew to a halt and looked inside. There, they saw their friend, looking strangely sinister under the light of a bare light bulb hanging from the ceiling. She was holding something up to the light – a syringe full of a pale liquid.

"Paula! Paula, stop," Izzy cried out as she drew back the bolt to the stable.

"Izzy... Kate... what are you doing here?" And now that Paula was talking and smiling, she didn't look sinister any more. She looked the way she usually did – relaxed and friendly.

"What's that in your hand?" Izzy stepped into the box.

"Hand?" Paula looked surprised and laughed.

"Yes, behind your back," Izzy said.

"I don't have anything behind my back..."

"We're not falling for your pathetic story, Paula," Izzy said angrily. "You've got a syringe, don't you? You've been using us. You've been totally leading us up the garden path – all that nonsense about Ted being involved."

And now, as Izzy looked at Paula, she could see no warmth in her eyes – no kindness at all. It was as though she was a completely different person from the one they'd known.

"You were going to give Seattle something, weren't you?" Kate joined in.

"So you think you're going to stop me, do you?" Paula said coldly. "Nobody's going to stop me." She raised the syringe.

"Drop that, Paula." Sally's shocked face appeared

at the door to the stable. Carefully, she walked through the middle of Izzy and Kate and into the box. Courtney and Megan stood behind her in the doorway.

Seattle Surprise lashed out with her hindlegs against the rear of the box, but Paula didn't move a muscle. *"Drop that, Paula."* She imitated Sally's voice. "I'm not dropping anything – not for anyone..."

Paula's arm lunged forward to stab Seattle when, just at that moment, Courtney flung herself forward, knocking the syringe flying. Seattle started back, and there was a scuffle as the syringe fell and Courtney stomped it underfoot.

Paula stared at her in disbelief, and then back at the syringe.

"You... you've ruined everything," she said, crumbling to the floor. And now, as she buried her head in her hands, all they could hear were the racking sobs coming from her body.

Izzy looked at Sally, calming Seattle. It had all happened so quickly.

"It's all right, girls," she said. "I called security as soon as I saw there was a problem. They'll be here in a minute."

And, at that moment, two men appeared. "This girl has just tried to dope my horse," Sally said.

The men stepped forward and grabbed Paula's hands. Izzy would never forget the crumpled look on her face as she was led out of the stables...

*

The gates slammed open and the horses were racing for the Gresham Maiden Stakes.

Speeding cleanly out of the stalls, Seattle Surprise jostled with the other horses until finally she settled mid-field on the rails. Izzy tuned in to what the commentator was saying.

"And it's Silver Dollar who's kicked clear of the pack by two lengths. Racing quickly in the red is Sprightly Lad, Night Clown is tucked in behind these in third, and then Seattle Surprise is on the rails in fourth." Then there was a stream of names that Izzy didn't listen to.

"She's sitting nicely." Izzy heard Courtney murmur as the horses raced through the clubhouse turn.

Izzy looked at Sally. Her knuckles were as white as chalk as she gripped the sides of her binoculars. Silver Dollar was setting a stupendous pace, stretching the pack out, but Seattle wasn't far off the lead.

"Now they're through the first furlong," the commentator announced. "Serendipity is at the back of the field. But it's Silver Dollar who's increased his lead to three lengths from Sprightly Lad."

"Don't let them run away with you, Seattle." Izzy sounded worried.

"And it's Silver Dollar on the inside, Sprightly Lad in second and Night Clown is back in third," the commentator called. "Seattle Surprise is in fourth, and coming very fast in the pink sleeves is River Boy and then it's half a length back to Field of Dreams. They're racing very quickly now. Making headway is Seattle Surprise."

"Come on, Seattle," Izzy cried excitedly as she listened to the commentary.

"It's still Silver Dollar, half a length back is Sprightly Lad. Night Clown has faded back, and Seattle Surprise chases along in third. Moving up on the outside are River Boy and Field of Dreams."

"Don't get boxed in," Kate murmured in dismay as she realized the race was nearing the end and that there were two horses closing up on Seattle's outside.

"It's Silver Dollar and Sprightly Lad who have been joined by River Boy. Field of Dreams is on the outside of these and Seattle Surprise is trying to find an opening, but there's nowhere for her to go..."

The horses ran around the far turn.

"Come on, Seattle," Courtney murmured. "You can find a way through."

The crowd started cheering and Izzy gripped Kate's shoulder as she watched the little gray mare fighting for her ground. There could only be some three furlongs left. Izzy grimaced. It looked like an impossible task. She wasn't going to do it.

"And now Seattle Surprise is pulling wide," the commentator called. "Field of Dreams has faded away and Seattle Surprise is moving up into third – she's only some three lengths off the lead. And it's Sprightly Lad and Silver Dollar, racing neck and neck, with Seattle Surprise coming up to challenge them."

The four girls could hardly bear to watch. Seattle was quickening all the time but the winning line was getting closer and closer.

"Sprightly Lad still has the edge, but Silver Dollar is fading, and it's Seattle Surprise who challenges his lead. These two have settled down to fight it out."

"Come on Seattle... come on..." And now Izzy and Kate were jumping up and down.

"And what a remarkable recovery – it's Seattle Surprise and Sprightly Lad, racing neck and neck... too close to call! Stand by for the photo!" The horses flashed past the winning post and the infield board flashed up – *photo*.

"Do you think she got it?" Izzy and Kate said excitedly. They turned around, but Sally had already disappeared. Courtney and Megan stood there, looking worried.

"Did she get it?" Courtney said.

"I'm not sure now." Izzy felt nervous. "But did you see the way she found that extra spurt of speed to catch the leaders? She came from nowhere."

The girls tore across the grass, stopping only as Seattle Surprise was led off the track, waiting for the result.

Seattle's flanks were glistening with sweat, but her ears were pricked as the commentator called the result of the photograph – Seattle Surprise was indeed first; Sprightly Lad was second and Field of Dreams was third.

Izzy and Kate could hardly hear themselves speak as they jumped up and down, whooping with delight. They turned to Courtney and Megan, who looked ecstatic as they all linked arms, jumping up and down together.

"One thing's for sure this time," Izzy grinned. "There's not going to be any problems when the results of that test come back. Now come on, let's celebrate!"

18

ALL IS REVEALED

"To think that we came so close to losing it all..." Doug Bryant stood looking out over the paddocks at Graytops. He was a tall man with an open face and russet-red hair. "It's good to be back," he murmured, taking it all in. The corners of his mouth creased into a smile as he watched the yearlings chasing each other in play.

"And everything's going to be all right now, Doug." Sally walked over to join her husband and rested her hand on his shoulder.

Izzy and Kate didn't know what to say. It had only been yesterday that Seattle had won her race and Paula had confessed to everything, and yet already it felt like an eternity ago.

"You know, I never imagined for a moment that Paula could be behind it all," Sally deliberated, shielding her eyes from the sun. "She was always a little strange – all of those tall tales she used to tell – but to try to ruin us..."

"I don't think any of us could have imagined what she was up to." Doug breathed in slowly. "How could we have known what deep-rooted hatred she was harboring toward our family? I would never have guessed who her father was."

"No, neither would I." Sally looked thoughtful. "She doesn't even look like him and I certainly wouldn't have recognized her from the days her father was our stable manager. She was only a small kid back then."

Courtney and Megan moved closer to their parents, waiting for an explanation.

"We couldn't have done anything but fire Hal," Doug shrugged. "Not when we found out how much he was stealing from us. A more rational person wouldn't have held us responsible for him starting to drink, but then I suppose it did cause the break-up of Paula's parents' marriage, and then when her younger sister was killed in that terrible car crash – well, I guess she needed someone to blame. I have to say I do feel pretty sorry for her – she hasn't exactly been given the easiest of lives..."

"Sorry?" Courtney and Megan looked surprised, while Izzy and Kate looked aghast. "How can you feel sorry for Paula after everything she's done? The way she tried to dope the horses – even breaking and entering Graytops at night!"

"Paula's obviously not well," Doug said firmly. "And hopefully she can get some sort of psychiatric help now. All I want is for Graytops to get back to normal. And now that everyone knows I wasn't doping

128

the horses and my suspension's been lifted, it shouldn't take us long. We could find we have a very busy future ahead of us. And it's all thanks to Izzy and Kate here that we even have that future."

Izzy and Kate squirmed uncomfortably. Neither of them had told the Bryants the full extent of their involvement with Paula. If they didn't come clean now, then they never would.

"Um, well, look... Doug and Sally. Actually, we've got a little confession to make." Izzy looked across at Kate, and Kate nodded. "We hate to admit it, but we really liked Paula. We didn't have any idea she could be behind it until the last minute." Izzy took a sideways glance at Sally, waiting for reassurance. "As you know, we thought it was Ted." It was all out in the open now... there was no going back.

"Me?" It was Ted's turn to look surprised.

"But only because that's what Paula wanted us to believe," Izzy added hurriedly. "I know it sounds crazy but we thought you were working for Joe Hagan."

"Joe Hagan? But what's he got to do with any of this?" Doug looked surprised.

Kate looked embarrassed. "It just seemed too much of a coincidence to us that Joe Hagan's horses came in second on both occasions-"

"And then when we found out that Joe had Ted's mobile number, it convinced us that he had to be the missing link – that Joe must be using Ted to do his dirty work for him." Izzy looked sheepish. Even as she said it, she knew it sounded silly.

Ted looked shocked. "But Joe's just a friend – there wasn't anything sinister about him having my mobile number."

"We know that now," Kate said.

"It does seem as though you put two and two together and came up with five." Sally stepped in hastily to defuse the situation. "But luckily everything's worked out for the best."

Izzy thought hard – there was something still bothering her – something at the back of her mind. But what was it? Of course – Ted's telephone conversation. *'I'll fight you every step of the way... I can't get you that kind of money... but that would kill her.'* What had that all been about? "Our suspicions weren't totally without grounding though," Izzy started tentatively. "You see, we did overhear this telephone conversation of Ted's."

"You mean the telephone conversation when I caught you eavesdropping?" Ted said angrily.

"Yes, but... but..." Izzy stammered.

"Yes, well I was talking to my ex-wife," Ted said. "The last couple of months haven't exactly been the easiest for me – what with the custody hearings for my daughter and everything – my wife wanted to take her to New York State to live."

"Oh..." Izzy and Kate didn't know what to say.

"Still, it's all right now," Ted said gruffly. "My daughter's staying."

"Your daughter's staying?" Courtney and Megan cried excitedly.

"Yeah," Ted's face relaxed. "My wife's realized that Andrea needs her father too."

"We're really sorry we suspected you," Izzy said.

"Well," Ted hesitated. "I suppose I have been acting a little strangely since you girls got here, so let's put it behind us."

Kate and Izzy looked at each other. It was the first time they'd seen Ted smile. It was hard to believe, looking at the changed man in front of them, that they'd ever really suspected him. How could they have been so stupid?

"Everything that Paula did – it just doesn't bear thinking about, does it?" Courtney said, shivering as she moved closer to her parents and slipped an arm around her mother's waist.

"Still, everything's going to be just fine now." Sally gave Courtney a hug and ruffled Megan's hair. She turned to Izzy and Kate and smiled. "I'm sorry all this has been going on while you've been out here – it hasn't been much of a vacation for you, has it?"

"Oh, but we've had a good time, haven't we, Kate?" Izzy said. "It's certainly been – well, different anyway."

"You've been fantastic." Doug stepped in. "I can't thank you enough for all your hard work."

As the Bryant family stood together, Izzy and Kate felt a little awkward. They didn't know what to say.

Courtney and Megan turned around and smiled at them.

"You know we'll miss you when you're gone," Courtney said. "It'll be kind of quiet. Maybe you two could come back to stay at Graytops some other time?"

"Yeah, well, you'd have to promise not to put us to work again!" Izzy laughed.

"Of course," Megan grinned. "But first of all we've got a summer at Sandy Lane to look forward to next year."

"Yeah, and hopefully a quiet, restful one at that!" Courtney exclaimed.

"Quiet?" Izzy laughed, slowly considering Courtney's words. She supposed that anything would seem quiet after the goings-on at Graytops, but *restful*?

"Yeah, and restful," Courtney teased. "That's just what we'll be looking for."

"Well, if that's what you want, we'll have to see what we can provide!" Izzy nudged Kate and muttered under her breath. "Don't spoil the illusion for them!"

Horse in Danger by Michelle Bates

The seventh title in the Sandy Lane Stables series

Rosie couldn't see anything, but she could definitely *hear* something. The barn door in the far corner of the yard was shut, both sections of the door bolted tightly. Rosie didn't know why, but suddenly she felt very nervous.

Taking a deep breath, she crossed the yard and walked over to the stable. Hesitantly, she reached up to pull back the bolt and slide open the door. As she did so, a hand plunged forward and grabbed her into the darkness...

Rosie and Jess have always been the greatest of friends, but more recently they've found themselves drifting apart. On the Autumn Treasure Hunt Ride, Rosie sets out to make amends. But what she discovers that day takes her down a path of deception and danger, putting her friendship with Jess to the ultimate test.

The Perfect Pony by Michelle Bates

The eighth title in the Sandy Lane Stables series

The stable yard was already busy that
morning and there was a crowd of people
gathered around the barn in the corner.
Horses and ponies whinnied loudly, and
the sound of crashing hooves on timber
echoed around the stable yard. Before
Alex even had a chance to walk over,
Tom had crossed the stable yard toward
him.

"I wouldn't like to be in your shoes
right now, Alex..."

Sandy Lane Stables is having difficulties – three
of the ponies are lame. Alex Hardy thinks he's got
the perfect solution to the problem, but soon finds
that he's let himself in for a whole lot more than he
bargained for...